2.50

MOD

033

Elizabeth Taylor (1912–75) was born in Reading, Berkshire, and educated at the Abbey School. She worked as a governess and librarian before her marriage in 1936. She spent most of her adult life in Penn, Buckinghamshire, and had two children. Elizabeth Taylor wrote many novels and short stories and is increasingly regarded as one of the best British writers of the twentieth century. *Mossy Trotter*, first published in 1967, is her only children's book

Mossy Trotter

ELIZABETH TAYLOR

ILLUSTRATED BY TONY ROSS

virago

VIRAGO

This edition published in Great Britain in 2015 by Virago Press
First published in Great Britain in 1967 by Chatto & Windus Ltd

1 3 5 7 9 10 8 6 4 2

A CIP catalogue record for this book
is available from the British Library.

ISBN 978-0-34900-557-7

Typeset in Goudy by M Rules
Printed and bound in Great Britain by
Clays Ltd, St Ives plc

Papers used by Virago are from well-managed forests
and other responsible sources.

MIX
Paper from
responsible sources
FSC
www.fsc.org
FSC® C104740

Virago Press
An imprint of
Little, Brown Book Group
100 Victoria Embankment
London EC4Y 0DY

An Hachette UK Company
www.hachette.co.uk

www.virago.co.uk

From the Writer's Son

My mother wrote many books for adults, but only this one for children, and some of it is based on my childhood. When I was growing up I didn't notice how much time she spent writing. She did most of it when my father was at work and my sister and I were at school or playing outside. When we came home she would quietly put her exercise book to one side and serve our tea or run a bath.

I suppose that most writers draw on real life as inspiration for their stories. My mother always carried a notebook when she was out: she was a very good eavesdropper and would write down bits of conversations she overheard on the bus or in a café to 'use' some time in a future book. She must have made notes of things that I got up to because you'll read about some of my adventures in *Mossy Trotter*. Most of these stories are true – like Mossy, I also played with tar, ruining my clothes, and my mother threatened to cancel my birthday party, too!

So, a word of warning. If you see your mother quietly writing in a notebook when you have been naughty, she might be planning to write a book – and the stories just might be about you! You never know. I didn't! I was probably about your age then, and now I am old enough to wonder what my grandchildren must think of their grandfather being such a naughty boy!

We lived at the end of a quiet lane on the edge of a big town in Buckinghamshire. There are now houses where the rubbish dump – my paradise – once was, and a motorway goes through the middle of the woods where we built our camps. Emma, Mossy's sister, is based on my little sister, Jo. She wasn't allowed to play in our gang because she was three years younger and a GIRL! She was too much of a baby to play real bows and arrows or to swing like Tarzan from a rope on a tree. The story about Mossy and Emma lost on the common reminds me of the evening when my best friend and I hid in the woods to worry our parents – we only gave ourselves up when we heard the voice of the village policeman who had been called to help in the search.

On the VERY rare occasion that I was especially naughty I would be sent to my bedroom. A couple of years ago I was moving some furniture that had been handed down by my parents and I happened to open a chest of drawers. Inside, I found a pencil drawing of a man's head, with lots of dots hovering over it. Beneath, in childish writing, were the words 'John Taylor has fleas'. It was how I took revenge on my father when I was a boy – more than sixty years ago!

I do hope that you enjoy this book.

And I wonder if you can walk past a recently repaired pot-hole without putting your toe in the shiny wet tar to see if it is still sticky?

I can't!

Renny Taylor, 2014

To
HARRIET ROUTLEDGE
and also to
VENETIA ERCOLANI
who asked me
to write it

Contents

1

Visit of Miss Silkin

'It's a *paradise* for children,' Miss Vera Silkin said, standing under the lilac tree by the gate, and looking across the common. Mossy knew what the word 'paradise' meant. It was a place like heaven. And he wondered how Miss Silkin could know that it was heaven.

Standing where she was she could not possibly see the beautiful rubbish dump among the bracken. This had been his private paradise from the moment he discovered it. It was a shallow pit filled with broken treasures from which, sometimes, other treasures could be made. People had thrown away old bedsteads and rusty bits of bicycles, tin cans, battered coal-buckets for making space helmets from. If he could only find two odd wheels, he could build himself a whole bicycle, he thought. And every afternoon when he came home from school, he went to the rubbish dump to see if there were any luck.

He had just come back from there to find Miss Silkin standing at the gate with his mother. 'Oh, a *paradise*,' she said again, in her silliest voice.

She was one of the friends they had had in London, and had come down to see their new house in the country.

'You lucky little boy,' she said to Mossy, putting her hand on his head – a thing he hated people to do, especially her. He knew by that steady look on his mother's face that he simply had to stay still and bear it. To wriggle away from Miss Silkin would be rude.

'And *you're* a lucky little *girl*,' Miss Silkin said to Mossy's sister, drawing her up close to her, which little Emma did not seem to mind at all. She was a cuddly little pudding. She liked to sit on people's laps and be petted. She was only four and did not go to school yet.

There were two of them – Mossy and Emma – and another on the way. 'There's another one on the way,' Mossy sometimes told people; but it had been such a long time on the way – since back in winter, it seemed – that he hardly ever thought about it now.

Although it was quite a warm day, Miss Silkin was wearing her usual furs round her neck – two long, thin dead animals with yellow glass eyes in their heads. Mossy wondered if they had once upon a time been rats. One head peeped over Miss Silkin's shoulder, and little paws hung limply down her back. Mossy hated these furs. They smelled of camphor, and looked shabby. He crept behind Miss Silkin's back and pulled faces at them; until he saw his mother looking at him again, with the same look. *She* was trying to make two faces at once – one to tell him to behave himself, and the other to show Miss Silkin that nothing was happening, that she was just listening and listening to her going on about paradise.

They went up the path under the cherry-trees and in through the front door. Emma was still clinging

lovingly to Miss Silkin's skirt. As if she actually *liked* her, Mossy thought.

Tea was laid out in the sitting-room. Tiny cucumber sandwiches – each one just a mouthful – and a cake with little black seeds in it. This was Miss Silkin's favourite. Mother always made one when *she* came to tea. Mossy wouldn't eat it. It had an old-fashioned smell, like Miss Silkin's furs.

He was sent to wash, and he stood at the sink in the kitchen, turning the soap over and over in his hands, getting his shirt-sleeves wet, and he was wondering to himself how long Miss Silkin would be staying. He would rather be out here, washing his hands, than go into the sitting-room to be asked all those questions like, 'How are you getting on at school?'

On other days, when he came home from school and had returned from inspecting the rubbish dump, he and Emma would have baked beans on toast at the kitchen table, and Mother would sit with them, sipping her cup of tea; and the only question *she* ever asked Mossy was what he had had for school dinner. She always wanted to know that, and when he said 'Sausages and cake', she would click her tongue, as if she thought sausages and cake were no good at all. Once, he said, 'Shepherd's pie without much shepherd,' and she had laughed, and told his father when he came home from work. Mossy always made that

joke now, and sometimes she laughed and sometimes
she didn't.

Father came home when they had finished tea, and
were just sitting round doing nothing. Well, all they
were doing – Miss Silkin and Mother – was talking.
Mossy was picking at a scab on his knee. Under the
scab was bright pink shiny skin, rather sore. 'Don't do
that, Mossy,' Mother kept saying. 'Did you hear what I
said, Mossy?' He heard all right, but couldn't resist it.
Then the scab came off suddenly, hurting smartly. He
yelped with pain. 'I told you,' his mother said. He put
the scab in his pocket and felt ashamed.

'How nice! How *very* nice!' his father said, hurrying

across the room towards Miss Silkin, as if he could not spare another moment to be near her. His voice sounded untrue. It was the voice he used when people 'dropped in', as he called it – just when he was going to have an evening mowing the lawn, or doing a crossword-puzzle, or having lots of little catnaps in front of the television – all things he loved doing. ('*Asleep*,' he always said in an astonished voice. 'I just dozed off for a second. It was so small I would call it a kitten-nap.')

He shook Miss Silkin eagerly by the hand, then he lifted the lid of the teapot and saw there was nothing inside.

'Shall I make some fresh?' Mother asked in a tired voice.

'No, no, old dear.' He took a cucumber sandwich and put it whole into his mouth, a thing Mossy had been told not to do. 'Seedy cake, ha!' he said. But he didn't take any of that. He hated it as much as Mossy did.

'And how's London?' he asked Miss Silkin – with his mouth full, Mossy noted.

Father never went there now that his job had brought them to this part of the world. He worked in the nearby town. He was a schoolmaster at the Secondary Modern. The fact that he was a schoolmaster made it seem extra hard to him that Mossy was not very clever at his lessons. Sometimes he tried to help him with his sums, but Mossy fidgeted and said,

'Oh, *we* don't do it *that* way.' And they got cross with one another.

'London's fine,' Miss Silkin said, as if it were all her doing that it was.

Mossy had liked some things about London – the red buses, and the parks. But here was better. It was *all* park. He had liked the super-markets, too, with the big wire baskets on wheels. He would push them round for Mother, and urge her on to take more and more things from the shelves, to stock up the basket. Then she would suddenly realize that she had spent far more than she had meant to, and rather shamefacedly would put a lot of the things back where they had come from.

'Can I put the television on?' Mossy asked.

'No, dear,' his mother said. 'We have a visitor.'

'Don't you have any homework to do?' asked Miss Silkin.

'Well, it's Friday, so I can do it tomorrow. Or the next day.'

'Then it will be hanging over you all the weekend,' she pointed out nastily.

It was so true, but if he did it this evening it would spoil the nice thing about Friday – the lovely free feeling which made it different from all the other weekdays. 'Looks as if she'll be hanging over me all the weekend, too,' Mossy thought gloomily.

'Well, this won't do,' Father said. 'I must do *my* homework.' He took up a pile of exercise-books and went bounding out of the room with them, as if he were looking forward to the job.

Mossy wandered out of the house and along the track. He looked through the bars of the gate when he came to his friend Selwyn's house, but there was no sign of life there, and he could hear the dog whimpering inside the house, so he knew they must be out. Selwyn's was the last house on the common. After that, there were just gorse bushes and juniper bushes and beech-trees, and deep glades and thickets where it was easy to get lost.

He was just moving away from Selwyn's gate when he was horrified to hear Miss Silkin's voice quite close by. He put his face to the bars again and looked through – as if he thought that she would not see him if he did not see her. But she had noticed him already, in fact she had come hurrying after him.

'I thought we could go for a little stroll while Emma's being bathed,' she said. 'Isn't it rather rude to stare into people's gardens?'

'It's my friend's,' Mossy said.

'Oh, well. That poor dog yelping like that. They *have* got mildew on their rose bushes.'

Mossy thought *she* was staring now, and in a very rude way, too. He moved off along the common, scuffing his feet in some grit where the track faded out into the springy turf.

'I shouldn't do that,' Miss Silkin said, following him. 'After all, someone's got to clean your shoes, and buy you new ones when those are worn out.'

His steps always led him to the rubbish dump, and Miss Silkin was horrified. She put her handkerchief to her nose and said the place was an eye-sore and shouldn't be allowed, and Mossy was to come away from it at once before he caught all sorts of germs. He gave a quick glance to see if there were anything new, anything added since before tea-time; but there hadn't been anything new for many days. However, as they wandered on he found in some bushes an old bicycle mud-guard. It must have been dropped on the way to the dump. Although it was rusty, it was better than the one he had got, and he pounced on it with joy.

'For goodness sake!' said Miss Silkin. 'Put that filthy thing down this minute.'

'It's just what I wanted,' he said, beginning now to want it more and more.

'Goodness knows where it's been,' she said.

Where things had been was what grown-ups worried about all the time. Where the germs came from, they thought; and sure enough, Miss Silkin said, 'It's probably covered with germs.'

Mossy did as he was told, but he was cross all the way home, for Miss Silkin, not at all liking this part of the common, turned round and began to walk back.

When they reached home, Emma had been put to bed, but they could hear her upstairs droning away, telling herself a story.

'*You* should wash your hands,' Miss Silkin told Mossy. Then she began a long complaint to Mother about the disgraceful rubbish dump. She goes on and on, thought Mossy. He could hear some of her words above the splashing of the kitchen tap. 'Infested with flies ... rats, too, most likely ...' 'Council should take steps.' On and on. Mossy put his hand over the tap and let it come out in little gushes. The front of his shirt was sopping wet.

'Stop playing with the water,' Mother called out from the next room. Playing with water was another sin.

He dried his hands and dabbed at his shirt with the roller towel. Then he went upstairs. His father did his work in a little spare bedroom. He could shut himself in there and correct his exercise-books and prepare lessons for the next day. Mossy thought he worked very hard.

He opened the door quietly and peeped inside. Father had his feet up on the table. He was leaning back in his chair, smoking his pipe, and reading one of his photography magazines. He grinned when he saw Mossy. He took the pipe out of his mouth and pointed with it to the floor – through the floor they could hear Miss Silkin's voice still going on and on. '*Such* a disgrace,' she was saying. 'Ruining the countryside. You should do something, Laura.'

Mossy grinned back at his father.

'There's often a funny side to things,' his father said.

2

The Dreadful Threat

Like many mothers, Mossy's was rather changeable. He could not always be sure where he stood with her. Although she tried very hard never to break promises, she broke threats, which in a way are a kind of black promise. She would send Mossy to his bedroom for having misbehaved, and then in a minute or two, tell him he could come down; or he would be told that if he were naughty he could not have chocolate cake for tea, and be given it for supper instead. It was a shocking way to bring up children, he once heard his father say.

But the threat about playing with the tar he truly believed. It was the sternest threat he had ever had, and he knew his mother was at the end of her patience when she made it. He had been warned and punished over and over again, but still he could not resist the temptation.

Their garden gate opened straight on to the common. There was a rough track, where neighbours' cars and trade vans could drive along, and then the springy turf and the bracken and the gorse and juniper bushes. At this time of the year, the gorse was covered with golden blossom and the beech-trees were still in pale, thin leaf which the sun shone through. It was an enormous common, with dells and glades and grassy walks. In some parts, trees grew in circles and inside these Mossy and his best friend, Selwyn, made camps and played games. On that common it was very easy to get lost.

At the end of the cart-track, a lane led away towards the village and this early summer men were tarring the surface. The tar, with its beautiful smell and its warm oozy softness, acted like a magic spell on Mossy and Selwyn.

After the first row at home when they had played stamping in the tar and spoilt their clothes, Selwyn was wise enough to keep away; but Mossy could not. In many ways, Selwyn had more sense than he.

Mossy would hang about in the garden, or visit the rubbish dump, or swing on the gate; but the smell of that tar, wafting towards him on the warm air, and the sound of the steam-roller trundling up the lane, drew him in the end.

He would just watch, he thought, just for a minute or two, well out of harm's way. He would just go to find out how far they'd got with the work.

And to begin with, he would stand in the tar-splashed grass at the side of the road; then he would drop a few stones on to the tar to see if they stuck; then he would put out his toe and prod an oozy patch, and in no time at all he was stamping in it, picking bits up and rolling them into rubbery balls, and his legs would be smeared, and so would his jeans and his shirt.

When he got home, there would be another horrible row. His mother would scrub him with a rag soaked in eucalyptus-oil until he was sore. The tar-marks would fade from black to pale brown and then disappear from his skin as his mother rubbed, and all the time she was rubbing she was ticking him off.

He wondered why he did it, as he sat on his bed in disgrace – sent upstairs for punishment. He waited for his mother to call him down again, but for once she didn't. That was the trouble with her. You couldn't ever be quite sure.

'How many times have I to tell you? Just look at this shirt.' On and on she had grumbled. Then she had said, 'If ever this happens again, you shan't have your birth-day party.'

The threat about the party was serious. His birthday was in fifteen days' time. He would be seven. He talked about it every day, although his father said it wasn't the thing to do. It was too much like reminding people to be sure to be in good time to buy him a present. And Mossy didn't think that such a bad idea either.

His birthday was the great day of the year, besides Christmas. It was his own day, when the magic of his importance lifted him above everyone else; when at school, he felt that the others were all thinking about *him* every minute of the day.

As the time went by, and his birthday drew nearer, his power grew, the power to choose who should come to his party.

Sometimes, he had quarrels with boys, and then he would tell them they wouldn't be invited. But by the next day, they would have made it up, and the party was on again for them. He was like his mother in this.

If he could not have a party, he knew that all this power would be gone from him. Besides that, he had talked so much about it. It would look as if he had boasted and told lies. His friends would sneer at him, or make fun. It would be enough to make him dread the day.

He felt a great sense of danger, and steered clear of the lane for a whole day. It was a little easier for him to do so, as the steam-roller was working farther away now, and the noise was not quite so loudly enticing; but the wafts of tar smell came every so often on a puff of wind.

On the next day, when he came home from school, there was a deep silence from the lane. He supposed the job was finished, and the steam-roller had trundled off somewhere else. He imagined the lane, smooth with its bright, new rolled-in gravel; and he thought it could do no harm now to go to have a look. All the dangerous tar would be covered over safely with gravel.

The lane was empty, and the sun beat down on the hot surface of the road. It looked very nice, now that it was finished, and all the pot-holes filled in. He took a stick from the hedge, and prodded at the tar. The stick sank into it. It was a pleasant feeling. He suddenly had the idea of running home and fetching the pair of stilts he had had for his Christmas present. He was quite good on them, and he would be able to walk perfectly safely right down the road on them, and there would be the delightful sensation of sinking crunchily into the tar with every step he took – just like the stick which he had prodded softly into the side of the road.

He threw the stick away and raced home.

'Nearly tea-time,' his mother called out from the kitchen.

'Just coming,' he shouted back, although he was really just going, with his stilts over his shoulder.

The lane was still empty. There was nobody about on this hot, quiet afternoon. He got up on to his stilts and took a step on to the beginning of the tarred road. It was just as delightful as he had thought it would be. The tar made little sucking noises as he carefully lifted the stilts – one after the other – from the gravel, and little stones got stuck to the ends of them.

The sun beat down, melting the tar, bringing up the smell of it. Mossy was blissfully happy. He went on very carefully, keeping the stilts straight, not letting them go too wide apart, or get out of his control. He passed one or two cottages, but there was nobody about to admire him. He was nearly at the other end of the lane when the disaster happened. The baker's van suddenly swept round the corner, with such a crunching and a scattering of gravel that Mossy looked up quickly. He faltered, he wobbled, he tried to keep his balance, tried to get to the side of the road, and fell.

When he got up, which he was too shocked to do for a moment or two, he went to pick up the stilts. Then he examined his knees. Tar was ground into them, and bright drops of blood rolled down on to his socks. There was tar on his shorts too, and on the elbow of his blazer.

This was worst of all. He had spoiled his precious school clothes. And there would be no party. He could imagine how the beastly eucalyptus would sting as his mother tried to clean up his grazed knees. And there would be no party.

He was done for now. Nothing could make matters

worse. With his stilts on his shoulder, he walked right down the middle of the road, whistling feebly with lips that he couldn't stop from trembling. 'I don't care,' he told himself, over and over again. 'I don't care.' But he did care. The bottoms of his sandals were now caked with tar, and little stones were embedded in them. They felt twice as heavy as usual, and so did his heart.

The row started as soon as he crept into the house. He was late, his mother called out. Where on earth had he been, she wanted to know.

'Very late,' Emma said, too.

She was sitting down, eating her tea, very prim and proper. She was eating beans. She picked them up one by one with her fat little fingers. She had disgusting table-manners, Mossy often said. She even picked up jelly. He didn't make any remark about it now, just stood there staring in front of him, waiting for the storm to break.

Then Mother looked up and saw him, and she took in a long, furious breath before she spoke.

'Don't think you're sitting down like that, my lad. Look at your school clothes. Just look at them. And what did I tell you? You know what this means, don't you?' she asked grimly.

'Yes.'

'No party.'

'No, I know.'

Emma shook her head, pretending to be sad. 'No party,' she said.

'You shut up,' Mossy told her.

'Don't you dare to speak to your little sister like that. *And* when you're in such disgrace. Take those sandals off at once. Oh, dear!' Suddenly, she looked dreadfully tired, and she put her hand to her forehead as if it were aching. And this made Mossy sorrier than ever. He was quite glad when she seemed to buck up and get angry again.

He took off his sandals and put them outside the back door, and went upstairs to the bathroom. His grazed knees were very sore, and he dreaded his mother touching them. But when she did – although her lips were tight-shut in an angry line – she was quite gentle and patient and didn't hurt too much.

Then she took his dirty clothes and stalked off with them, and told him to go to his bedroom and get into bed, and to look sharp about it, too.

He kept making gulping noises as he undressed, trying not to cry.

When he had been in bed a little while, his mother came up the stairs with a tray. On it was a glass of milk and a plateful of cold beans on cold, soggy toast – all part of the punishment. The beans were gluey, and each one almost choked him. Tears met them at the back of his throat and he swallowed them together. Beans and misery, he thought. Yet he ate them all, and left a clean plate. He had had enough trouble for one day. Besides, he was surprisingly hungry. It was very odd, he thought, to have a broken heart and such an appetite, at the same time.

'You've gone to bed before me,' Emma said, in a sing-songy, jeering voice, putting her head round his bedroom door.

'Emma!' Mother called sharply.

However badly he was being punished, she would not allow gloating from anyone.

As soon as Mossy woke the next morning, he remembered that something was wrong; then he remembered what it was, and was filled with gloom. He could hear the cuckoo calling out somewhere on the common. It was one of his favourite sounds, but today it only added to his sadness.

Mother had come in on her way to bed, and had put his blazer and shorts on a chair. She must have spent a long time trying to get them clean – and in fact they weren't quite clean.

Mossy got up and dressed. It was better to be doing something than just lying in bed feeling miserable. When he was brushing his hair, he stared into the looking-glass, and put a stern expression on his face, and said – just as he was going to say to Selwyn and the others later – that he had decided against having a party this year. At his age, he had seen the last of them. And parties were girls' stuff anyway.

Then he asked himself what were a few old presents, anyway? It was a pretty mean thing – that, if you give a party, your friends bring presents; if you *don't* give a party, precious few of them ever bother.

At breakfast, nothing was said about his punishment. His mother added to the gloom, though, by passing round a picture postcard from Miss Silkin. It had a very bright blue sky pictured on it, and some palm trees. She was on a cruise. (Good! thought Mossy.) But she wrote that she had something important to tell them, and would come to see them as soon as she got back. (Bad! thought Mossy.) Father didn't say anything. He was frowning at some bills, which he crammed into his pocket, looking as if he didn't know what else to do with them.

Mossy went off to school, and tried out his speech first on his friend, Selwyn. Selwyn was much smaller than Mossy. He was in a class with older boys because he was clever for his age. He wore spectacles, which helped him to look more than ever like a wise owlet.

When Mossy said his speech about parties being fit only for girls, Selwyn blinked through his spectacles and said: 'Then I won't bother to ask you to mine in August, if you don't like them.'

'Won't worry me,' said Mossy; but he became quiet. This was something he hadn't thought about. He wouldn't be asked back to other people's parties. The punishment would go on and on.

When he reached home from school that afternoon, he said to his mother, 'Well, I told them I wasn't going to have a party.'

All she said was, in a careless voice, 'They had to know some time, hadn't they?'

Father came home very gloomy and, instead of going upstairs to correct the exercise-books, he sat at the kitchen table and went through bills.

Mossy stayed in his own garden to play. He had had enough of Selwyn for one day. He gave Emma rides in his truck, which was a wooden box from the grocer's, on wheels.

Whenever he wandered into the kitchen, his father was sighing over his bills, and all the money he had to pay.

'And with another one on the way,' he said, meaning the coming baby. Then he used some rude language about the income tax, and said to Mother, 'Must cut down, you know, old girl.'

This, Mossy knew, meant spending less money,

'I can't think how,' Mother said.

'Taxed to the hilt,' Father groaned – whatever it might mean. Mossy didn't know. Well, they were saving on his party, he thought. All those cakes and sandwiches and balloons.

Then he grew sad. There was always this trouble in the house about money, and always would be, he guessed – especially with another one on the way, another mouth to feed. There would have to be a bigger tin of baked beans at tea-time, and so on. So he would never get his bicycle. Bicycles cost a fortune, he had often been told; and there was no chance of a fortune coming to this family.

Mother took Emma up to bed, and then Father was left alone adding up figures, and sighing.

Mossy could not bear it any longer, so he went down to the village shop, and spent all the pocket-money he had left on a choc-ice. Then he ran all the way back with it, before it could melt, and gave it to his father.

It made a marvellous change in him. He ate it with great enjoyment, and cheered up immediately, just as Mossy would have done himself. Then he pushed all the bills on one side and said, 'Let's go for a walk on the common.'

So they set off, and went the same way as Mossy had walked the evening with Miss Silkin and, although that rusty mud-guard had long since been picked up by someone else, Mossy did find an old bicycle lamp, which was almost better; and his father made no silly speeches about germs.

One evening a little later, when Mossy was fast asleep in bed, Mother was sitting knitting a baby's jacket, and Father was doing a crossword-puzzle. They had just had a rather extravagant supper of veal and mushrooms and noodles, finishing with hot blackcurrant tart and very cold whipped cream, and they were quite happy in their way, and hadn't thought about the bills all the evening.

Only one small thing was worrying Mother. It was a little problem she knew she could put right in the end, but she couldn't think of the best way of doing it, and she was rather ashamed of telling Father.

'Robert,' she said, keeping her head down and knitting away.

He wrote something in his crossword-puzzle and said, 'Um-hum.'

'It's that party of Mossy's.'

'What about it?'

'Well, I told him he couldn't have it.'

'Why?'

'When he got that tar all over him.'

'Well, then he can't have it.'

Father got up and began to look for his pipe.

'The trouble is I'd already mentioned it to some of the mothers.'

'You shouldn't make empty threats, you know. I'm always telling you.'

'I know. But there was nothing else left. And I felt sure his party meant so much to him, that he wouldn't do it.'

'Well, you're in a bit of a fix, then, aren't you?'

'Yes. What do you think I ought to do?'

As he passed behind her chair, still searching for his pipe, he bent down and kissed her on the top of her head.

'You'll have to fight your own battles, old girl,' he said. Which wasn't much help to her.

She had been worrying about this problem for days. *She* was being punished, too; and it was no easier for her that she had only herself to blame. This is the trouble with punishments. They spread and spread. And there's not much to be done about it, once they're started.

Next day, Mother said to Mossy, at tea-time before Father came home, 'Well, I've been thinking, Mossy. As you've been a good boy, and haven't been near that tar since you were so naughty, I'm going to change my mind, and let you have the party. We really shouldn't punish the other children because of your behaviour. So we'll forget about your disobedience and have the party, after all.'

'I don't want it,' Mossy said.

'Why not?'

'I told them I think parties are silly. Only for girls.'

'But you were looking forward to it so much.'

'Well, I'm not now.'

Here was a fix for both of them. Everything was turned upside down. Once he had wanted the party and she had said he couldn't have it. Now she wanted him to have it; but, because of the things he had said about the babyishness and girlishness of birthday parties, he couldn't see how he could suddenly seem to have changed his mind about everything.

He was in such a muddle, he went round to see Selwyn.

'I'm wondering about that old party,' he said.

But Selwyn was no help.

'I think you're right,' he said. 'I reckon when I'm seven, I won't have one, either.'

It was all right for him. He still had his sixth birthday to come. And Mossy wasn't going to be asked to it.

Now, as the birthday drew nearer, Mother became more and more anxious. She began to suggest all sorts of enticements to Mossy – bigger and better balloons, a treasure-hunt in the garden, and little cakes with his friends' names iced on them.

All Mossy said was, 'What about that chap called

Octavius? You'd have to have a huge cake to ice that one on.'

The next day his mother was desperate.

'You can't punish other children, and take their party away from them, just because *you* were naughty.'

'No,' said Emma accusingly.

'Shush,' said Mother to her, impatiently.

'It was your idea I shouldn't have it,' Mossy said stubbornly.

'What a way to bring up children,' his father said, who for once had overheard the discussion.

He said this later to Mother when they were alone, and Mossy did not know about that.

In the end, Mossy gave in. It was quite simple.

He handed out the invitations at school.

'You are invited to a Party,' the cards had printed on them, and there was a picture of children carrying balloons.

'I thought you weren't going to have a stupid old party. I thought you said parties were for girls,' said Octavius, who was the eighth child of his family, and very spoilt and rather sneery.

'My mother made me,' Mossy said.

*

It was one of the very best parties in the end. The top
of the birthday-cake was decorated like a maypole, with
different coloured ribbons going out to the side of the
cake from a ribbon-bound stick in the middle – which
was really one of Mother's knitting needles; but she had
plenty of spare ones so that she could go on with the
baby's jacket. It was a cake that was long remembered
and talked about.

Mother, who broke her threats, broke none of the
promises, and there was a treasure-hunt, and bigger and

better balloons, and she even managed to cram the name *Octavius* on one of the little cakes, though the writing, in pink icing, got very cramped and small towards the end, and had to go down the side of the cake.

3

Miss Silkin's News

You may remember that Miss Silkin on her postcard had written that she had some special news to tell them about her cruise.

'What is a cruise?' Mossy asked his mother, thinking about this some days later.

'It's a holiday on a ship, visiting places, mostly abroad,' Mother said, and she went on, as if speaking to herself, that *she* would never manage to go on one now, especially with another baby on the way. Then she brightened up and said that she would much rather have the baby, and she thought of poor Miss Silkin who had none.

One afternoon, Mossy and his friend Selwyn had a very pleasant time making a house in one of the old cherry-trees in Mossy's garden.

The platform of the house was the bottom of Mossy's old truck. It had seemed to be time for it to be turned into something else. They fixed it up in the fork of the tree, and hung some sacking round it for walls, and the leaves of the cherry-tree made the roof. They had a rope-ladder hanging from one of the lower branches, and also an old basket that could be let down on a string. Emma, under the tree, put pieces of bread into it, and they hauled it up and ate the bread ravenously, and pretended that they had been starving for days, unable to get down the tree because wolves were roaming round underneath it. The bread was stale – some old crusts that Mother had thrown out for the birds; but the birds had preferred to eat the red-currants.

Through the leaves, they could see Mother coming in and out of the house, carrying things for tea. Then Mossy, peering through the branches, saw Miss Silkin coming out, too, carrying the teapot.

'Oh, *dear*!' he groaned to Selwyn, holding his stomach as if it ached.

'What's up?' asked Selwyn.

'You'll see.'

Mother called to them to come down from the tree, and they clambered down unwillingly, swinging to and fro on the rope until the palms of their hands felt as if they were on fire.

'See who's here?' Mother called gaily.

Miss Silkin was wearing a stiff white dress with a red anchor embroidered on the front. She gave Mossy a very peculiar look, as if she were seeing him for the first time. Her eyes were half-shut, and her head on one side. She was really studying him, and he felt awkward, and began to shuffle about.

'Selwyn may stay, if he runs and asks his mother,' Mossy's mother said.

'I asked her before I came. In case,' Selwyn said. 'And she said "yes".'

'Then both wash your hands and we'll have tea.'

Selwyn and Mossy went into the kitchen and rinsed off some of the tree dust, and Mossy peered into a small glass above the sink and wondered what was wrong with his face to have made Miss Silkin stare so much. He could see nothing out of the ordinary. He certainly hadn't suddenly grown another nose, nor had a hole gaped open on his forehead to let another eye look through – like some awful ogre.

They went back to the garden.

Father was away, playing in a cricket-match. (That was another thing that disappointed him in Mossy. It was bad enough his not being bright at lessons; but he liked climbing trees and making up his own games better than cricket. Sometimes in the evenings, Father would ask, 'Like me to bowl to you for a bit?' But it was

34

more like Mossy playing to oblige Father than the other way about.)

They sat down on the grass beside Emma, who was already picking currants out of a cake. As Miss Silkin had arrived unexpectedly there had not been time for Mother to make the special seed cake Mossy hated so much.

He and Selwyn ate tomato sandwiches quickly and quietly, and Miss Silkin kept turning her head to look curiously at Mossy, fidgeting as she did so with a big, glittering ring on her finger. He knew that something was up, and he didn't like it.

'May I tell them?' Mother asked her. She looked bright and excited.

'But of course.' Miss Silkin smiled and nodded.

'Miss Silkin is engaged to be married,' Mother said. 'Isn't that happy news?'

'What does "engaged" mean?' Emma asked.

'Well, darling, she has promised . . . '

'Herbert,' said Miss Silkin.

'She has promised Herbert to marry him.'

'I don't know any Herbert,' Emma said.

'You will,' Mother said.

'I'll bet we will,' thought Mossy.

'In the winter,' Miss Silkin said. 'We're going to be married in the winter.'

'But I don't *know* Herbert,' Emma whined, as if she were being left out of something.

'None of us knows Herbert – yet,' Mother said, still in the same bright voice, as if it were Christmas, or somebody's birthday.

'Yeah, he's her fiancé,' said Selwyn, who knew everything.

'And ... shall I break the news?' Miss Silkin asked Mother.

Mother's brightness went, like the sun suddenly going in, and she looked anxiously at Mossy, and then she nodded her head.

'We – that is, Herbert and I – want you, Mossy, to be our page-boy,' Miss Silkin said, staring hard at Mossy again, as if she were trying to imagine him dressed up, and with his hair combed.

Mossy went very red, and nearly choked on a piece of cake, and Selwyn laughed, and went on laughing, as if he had just heard the funniest joke of all his life. They both knew what being a page-boy meant. One of the boys at school – one of the very youngest ones – had had to be one, wearing velvet trousers and a frilled blouse.

'It's a *great* honour,' Mother said.

'Can *I* be one?' Emma asked.

'No, my darling,' Mother said. 'You're too little.'

'Then can I be next time, when I'm bigger.'

'Well, there won't be a next time,' said Miss Silkin, smiling fondly. Herbert, whoever he was, was going to last her for the rest of her life.

'Well, if *she's* too little, *I'm* too old,' Mossy began. He knew that he had to fight hard for himself now, and all alone. The two women – his mother and Miss Silkin – were against him; and his father was not there to help, and Selwyn was just gloating. 'Let Emma do it,' he went on desperately. 'If she wants to. I don't know how to. Anyway, I'm a boy.'

'That's what page-boys always are,' Miss Silkin said, and Selwyn gave another hoot of laughter. Mossy thought, That's the last time he comes *here* to tea.

'We'll talk about it later,' Mother said. 'When Father gets home. Won't you finish up the sandwiches, boys?'

But Mossy could not eat any more. He was in a dreadful panic.

'Where will the wedding be?' he asked.

'In London,' his mother said.

This was one mercy. If it were here in the village, all of his friends would see him. But Selwyn knew. It was a bit of bad luck that Selwyn knew.

'You see,' Miss Silkin went on, taking no notice of Mother's suggestion that they should talk about it later, 'my little niece, Alison, is just about your size, Mossy, and I thought the two of you would pair off so nicely as train-bearers.'

It was all terrible, and getting worse and worse to Mossy, who could imagine this Alison. Any niece of Miss Silkin's would be too much for him.

'Well, if we've all finished, would you boys like to help take the things inside?' Mother said.

Selwyn, smirking to himself while Mossy worried and fumed, had eaten the last sandwich. He got up and took a dish of biscuits, and managed to pop one into his mouth on the way to the kitchen. Mossy saw him do it. He wished Selwyn had gone to the other side of the world that afternoon, rather than come into his garden to play.

When Emma had been put to bed, and Selwyn had gone home at last, Miss Silkin wanted to show them the coloured slides she had taken on her cruise; so they set up Father's screen in the sitting-room and got out the projector, and drew all the curtains to keep out the light.

Father came home from his cricket-match, and had to be told Miss Silkin's news and look at her engagement ring. His face and neck were very sunburnt against his white shirt.

He sank down in a chair and waited for Miss Silkin to put on the slides. The first one was a ship upside-down with some upside-down seagulls flying round it.

'Oh, so sorry!' Miss Silkin snatched it out and put it in again the right way up. 'That's the dear old *Maid of Athens*,' she explained.

Which must be the name of the ship, Mossy decided.

The next slide was of some ship's rails, far from straight, and some more seagulls. The one after that was upside-down again. Mossy began to fidget.

Soon they were on dry land, and it looked very dry indeed. There was a picture of a banana tree.

'Anyone asleep yet?' Miss Silkin asked merrily. She meant the question as a joke; but in fact Father *was* asleep. And not only was he fast asleep, but nearly falling off his chair. Mossy watched him with interest for a while, waiting for him to fall with a crash. As this did not happen, he glanced back at the screen.

On the screen was a man wearing a bright shirt and a funny straw hat.

'Is that a native?' Mossy asked politely.

'No, it isn't,' Miss Silkin snapped. 'I was just about to tell you. That is Herbert. My fiancé.'

'He *looks* like a native,' Mossy said.

'Everyone is a native of *somewhere*,' Father said, waking up suddenly. '*We* are natives of England.'

'He looks *very* nice, Vera,' Mother said, leaning forward to see Herbert better.

'Has he got a beard?' Mossy asked.

'No, dear, I think that's just an unfortunate shadow,' Mother said. But Miss Silkin had taken the slide out, and seemed in quite a temper.

All the same, she went on and on showing them pictures of shabby old camels, and palm-trees, and market places, until the box of slides was empty. Then Father woke up again and said, 'Very nice! Very nice indeed!' and Mother said, 'Thank you, Vera dear,' to Miss Silkin and got up to draw back the curtains and let the evening sunlight in.

Miss Silkin this time was not staying overnight. She had a little blue car, very neat and tidy like herself, and soon after the projector had been packed away, she got into the car and drove off home to London.

When Mossy was in bed, his father came up to say 'goodnight', and Mossy told him of the dreadful plan Miss Silkin had for him.

'Sounds a bit rough,' his father said. 'But you'll have to do what your mother says.'

So Mossy knew that he was lost and done for. He knew that his mother loved him and she loved weddings, too; and to have them both mingled together would be the happiest of all things for her. She so loved everything about weddings, that often she would wait outside the church at ones she had not been invited to, and watch the bride coming out, and would tell them later what the bridesmaids wore, and that she didn't know who looked the prettiest, and no one cared but Emma.

Mossy remembered this now, and felt very panicky.

'But, Father, I'm too old,' he pleaded.

'I wouldn't know much about that,' Father said. 'It's

more in your mother's line. Well, and how many do you think your old Dad scored this afternoon?'

'I don't know,' Mossy said sadly.

'Forty-seven,' his father replied. 'Not so bad, even if I say so myself.'

He seems bright and bouncy enough, Mossy thought miserably, and he closed his eyes and looked stern, as though he would like to drop off to sleep, if only his father *would let him.*

4

Visit of Grandfather

As the days went by, Mossy began to forget the terrible wedding, as he thought of it; and he told himself that winter was a long way away, and anything might happen before then. Herbert might get fed up with Miss Silkin and refuse to marry her. This seemed more than likely to Mossy, and the more he thought about it, the more certain he became that it would happen.

Even Selwyn had at last forgotten and given up teasing him.

And then something put it entirely out of Mossy's mind. His grandfather came on a visit.

Mossy's real name was Robert Mossman Trotter. The middle name was after his Grandfather Mossman Trotter, and he was called Mossy to avoid muddling him with his father, who had the same name, Robert.

Grandfather was fat and jolly and smelled of beer. He had a red sports car, which people thought he was too old for. He drove it very fast, and Mother said he was a menace on the roads. He also had an old dog, called Fortnum, who sat beside him in the passenger's seat, panting and flapping his tongue with excitement. Fortnum was his only companion. They lived alone in a flat in London. Grandmother had died years ago, and Mossy could not remember her. 'Poor old Gertie,' Grandfather called her, when he was talking of the days gone by. 'That was when poor old Gertie was alive,' he often said.

Mossy was always glad to see him. The red car would come bumping down the common road, and pull up suddenly, scattering the gravel. Then Fortnum would follow Grandfather out of the car and up the path.

On this visit, he brought Mossy a bird book. There were beautifully coloured pictures of eggs – and a whole page of cuckoos' eggs, with the eggs of the foster-parents to compare them with.

'Artful customers, cuckoos,' Grandfather said. 'Never build a nest, just lay their eggs in some other bird's – and chuck out one of hers to make room. Dirty trick.'

But in spite of that, Mossy loved cuckoos. Their call from the far glades of the common was strange and beautiful to him. He sat at Grandfather's feet and looked at his bird book and was deeply contented.

Grandfather had brought a present for Emma, too. It was a little mug, very old, with a picture of two little girls in long dresses, and a boy with a black velvet jacket and cap, and a woman with a high bonnet. On one side of the mug there was a little poem.

> And when I learn my hymns to say,
> And work, and read and spell,
> I will not think about my play,
> But try and do it well.

'Belonged to poor old Gertie's grandmother,' said Grandfather.

'Oh, but it is *far* too valuable for a child,' Mother said, and put it on a high shelf out of Emma's reach, among other treasures. Emma began to cry, so Grandfather picked her up and gave her an aeroplane-ride across the room, holding her high above his head.

'You'll crash that child's head on the ceiling,' Father said. But Grandfather knew he never would, and so did Emma; and Mossy knew, too. He could remember his own aeroplane-rides – the delicious thrill of being zoomed across the room in Grandfather's arms, and ending up laughing on someone else's lap. He was too heavy for it now.

The next day – it was a Saturday – Grandfather took him for a ride in his car. The hood was down, and the wind blew his hair back from his forehead. He could smell all the country smells as they drove along the lanes – the scent of lime-blossom from the trees by the church, a cold, mushroomy smell as they drove through some woods, and the smell of the pigs at the farm.

In the nearby town, everyone was out shopping. Babies screamed in prams outside the shops and threw their toys overboard in tempers. Women pushed shopping-baskets on wheels straight through the crowds, with wicked glee. Pretty young girls rattled collecting-boxes under people's noses, selling flags.

When they had managed to park the car, Grandfather bought a flag from the prettiest girl, and she pinned it to his coat. They were quite gay together, as if they had known one another for years.

At the back of a cake-shop, there were a few tables where one could sit and drink coffee. On all of his visits, Grandfather took Mossy there for ice-creams. They went through the shop, which smelt deliciously of warm doughnuts, and sat down at one of the little tables. Grandfather ordered coffee for himself, and a strawberry and a chocolate ice for Mossy. He ate it very slowly from a little glass dish.

Grandfather did not seem at ease in this place. He pushed his chair back from the table, and stared about him at old ladies drinking coffee and nibbling biscuits. He smoked a cigarette, and kept glancing at his watch.

When Mossy had scraped up the last trace of ice-cream from the little dish, Grandfather got up and paid the bill, and they went out again into the busy street.

Grandfather stopped to pat one of the crying babies on the head and he picked up its rattle from the pavement; but the baby screamed louder than ever and went alarmingly red in the face, and its mother came darting out of the shop and glared at Grandfather.

'Let's get out of here,' he said.

They went to find the car and then drove into the quieter countryside.

In the village where Mossy lived, there was a little pub called *The Lamb and Flag*. It had a thatched roof and a creaking inn-sign with a picture of a baby lamb with a Union Jack in its mouth. There was a high, lumpy old hedge, full of birds' nests, and a little garden with trestle tables and benches set out under the apple-trees.

'Time for a pint,' said Grandfather, pulling up with a jolt outside the porch. 'You go through that little gate into the garden, there's a good lad, and I'll bring you out something nice to drink.'

Mossy thought what a lovely morning he was having – one treat after another. It was pleasant to be on his own with his grandfather, and he was glad Emma had not come. She might fidget in the car, and it would be a squash, Mother had said. There was not even room for Fortnum *and* Mossy.

He wandered round the garden. It was warm and peaceful there. Birds flew in and out of the hedge, and darted about the thatched roof, collecting insects. He sat down at one of the tables. It had been painted green, and there were blisters in the paint, but someone else had cracked them all.

Grandfather came out with their drinks on a tray. There was a very tall glass of ginger-beer and a packet of crisps for Mossy. It was blissful sitting there. A little striped cat came out of the pub and Mossy gave it a crisp; but it only sniffed at it and played with it.

'Better drink up,' Grandfather said in no time at all. His own glass was empty already. 'We'll be in hot water if we get back late for lunch.'

Mossy was worried now. He had most of the enormous drink still left, and he was horribly full-up. He struggled to get rid of some more, but he felt like a balloon. The ginger-beer fizzed and sparkled and went up his nose, and he kept gasping for breath as he drank. It was like trying to swallow a firework sparkler. But he was determined not to hurt Grandfather's feelings by leaving it.

High up in his chest was a very bad pain. Panting, he stared into the glass at the last of the soapy-looking drink and then, between hiccoughs, he gulped it down.

'Good show,' said Grandfather, getting up and making his way to the car. Mossy followed, staggering rather. He was silent on the way home, but Grandfather did not notice.

There was a smell of stew in the house when they got back. Mossy tried not to think about it, but it was soon time to sit down to lunch.

Father was home, because it was Saturday.

'Ah, stew!' he said, rubbing his hands.

('Ah, *stew!*' Mossy said to himself, not in such a happy way.)

'Poor old Gertie used to make a lovely stew,' said Grandfather.

A plateful was put in front of Mossy, and he stared at it, and sighed.

'Eat nicely,' Mother said to Emma, who was picking up pieces of carrot with her fingers. Mother seemed tired and cross, and her face was red from cooking.

Slowly, Mossy speared a piece of potato with his fork, and put it in his mouth. He swallowed it, then he had a little rest, leaning back in his chair.

'Eat up,' his mother said.

Her voice was very sharp today.

Although Mossy kept putting meat and vegetables into his mouth, the plateful stayed the same. It seemed that he could not make it grow less.

Grandfather was already having a second helping.

'Really, Mossy, do get on with it. Don't just sit there and let it grow cold,' said Mother. Then she looked at him suspiciously, and then even more suspiciously at Grandfather.

'Have you been filling him up with sweets? she asked.

'No,' said Grandfather truthfully.

'Because it's too bad if you have,' Mother said, as if she hardly believed him – 'Spoiling his appetite. Children need proper food, not a lot of rubbish. It really is too bad.'

She went on for some time, in a very annoyed voice, and Grandfather did not answer. He knew that it was no use denying again about the sweets. She would only find out that it was something else. So he sat very quiet, with his head bent, looking guilty, like a naughty child and Mossy hated to see him looking like that.

He suddenly sat up very straight, and said, 'Nothing's spoilt *my* appetite,' and he began to eat very fast and very bravely, for his grandfather's sake.

Mother leaned over, and cut up some meat on Emma's plate. She had stopped grumbling; but her face was now red from crossness, not cooking.

When Mossy's plate was clean, she got up and took the dishes to the kitchen, and came back with an apple-crumble. This was one of his favourite puddings. Sometimes, he hardly tasted the first helping for dreaming about the second. Today, he could not think at all about second helpings. He had to fix his mind on the first.

'Don't gobble so,' his mother said.

Well, really! he thought, for it seemed that he could do nothing right. He had been eating fast to get rid of it. And get rid of it he did. Although, in the end, he was afraid that he might cry, so upset and fussed he was, so sick and sorry for himself.

'Well, we know *one* who wants a second helping,' his father said, beaming at him.

Then they all looked at Mossy, who could only shake his head. He was afraid to speak.

When at last the dreadful meal was over, he got

down from the table and decided to go upstairs and lie down on his bed for a little, so that his stomach could digest the food in peace. Emma was already on her way up for her rest, and howling because she did not want to go. But until she was old enough for school, this is what she had to do, Mother said. It gave them all a breather, she explained.

As Mossy left the room, Grandfather put his hand on his shoulder, holding him tightly for a moment. 'Well done, and thank you,' he said in a low voice.

Mossy slowly climbed the stairs. He took his favourite book, which was *Charlotte's Web*, and he lay down on the bed, pulling the eiderdown cosily over him.

He discovered that, although he felt uncomfortable and queasy, it was still possible to be very happy at the same time. This surprised him.

As he read, he kept remembering what his grandfather had said. It interrupted the story, just as if it had been printed on the page. Before he had turned many of those pages, he had fallen asleep.

5

Lost on the Common

All through that very nice summer, Mossy, from time to time, thought about Miss Silkin's wedding.

One day, he stood outside the village church to watch a wedding-group being photographed. Although it upset him to look at this, he felt a horrible curiosity and fascination – the same feeling he had about an old war picture of dead horses in one of his father's books. When he was alone in the room, he was drawn towards that shelf where the book was, and he would open the book with trembling hands, and look at the picture, and wish he hadn't, and put it back.

This wedding-group was not so frightening and ugly as that picture; but it made him feel very uneasy. The bride had lots of red fuzzy hair, and she was laughing away as if this were the funniest thing that had ever happened to her. Mossy doubted that Miss Silkin would do that. He imagined *her* being proud and dignified. The bridegroom looked very pleased with himself – though Mossy could see no good reason for this. Worst of all were two children – a little girl with a wreath of flowers on her head and a pink sash round her fat stomach, and – horror of horrors – a page-boy dressed in velvet trousers and a frilly blouse.

The photographer made them stand hand-in-hand. They smiled in a sickly fashion. Then the photograph was taken at last, and people in the crowd threw paper rose-petals, and Mossy saw Selwyn coming along the road, so he hid behind two stout old women until he had passed.

He spent the rest of the afternoon with his friend Octavius, trying to fish a rusty can out of the village pond.

When he got back home, there was Miss Silkin herself to remind him of the scene outside the church. She had driven down from London, to have a chat about the wedding with Mother. They were sitting in the garden, looking at little snippets of material.

'And *this* one I thought for Alison's dress,' she was saying. Alison was to be the small bridesmaid.

'Nasty,' said Emma, because she was envious.

It was white silk with little blue rosebuds dotted over it.

'Oh, she'll look sweet,' Mother said, and then Emma began to grizzle, from the awful thought of someone other than herself being admired.

'Don't be silly,' Mother said. It was clear from her voice that Emma had been in one of her trying moods all afternoon.

'I wanted to be a bridesmaid. I'm never a bridesmaid.'

Mother was tired of explaining that she was too young, so all she said now was that little girls can't have everything they want.

'When *my* babies come, they won't have *anything* they want,' Emma said spitefully. She decided to get her own back on her children, if she could not on anyone else. 'I'm going to be very cross and strict with them. I'll keep smacking them. Smacking and smacking, all the time. I'll make them have liver every day. Every day, liver.'

'When *mine* come, I'm going to be very kind,' Mossy said. 'I'll never make them do anything horrible.' He looked very hard at his mother and Miss Silkin, and then he went on in a sing-song voice. 'They can have everything they want. *I'm* going to have very happy children. They can have bicycles, too. I shall save up for them.'

'You should start saving up for your own first,' Miss Silkin said snappily.

That reminded Mossy of the rubbish dump, and he

decided to go off at once and rake round there, and see what he could find.

'Where are you going?' his mother asked, as he made off.

'Oh, just on the common.'

'Me, too; me, too,' Emma began to whimper.

He moved faster towards the gate.

'Poor little pet,' Miss Silkin said soothingly to Emma.

'Please take her with you for a little walk,' Mother called out.

'There's a nice little brother,' said Miss Silkin. She put her hands over her ears, for she could not bear Emma's howling, and was thinking how pleasant it would be if the child went off for a little while, leaving Mother and herself in peace, so that they could have a good long talk about Herbert, and the wedding, and the dress materials.

'Oh, come *on* then,' Mossy said grudgingly.

'Hold her hand,' Mother called after them. 'And don't be long. It's nearly her bedtime.'

Emma was beaming now, as she trotted off towards the common, holding Mossy's hand. The sun had made her hair go very fair, in streaks, and her skin very dark. Miss Silkin had said, 'Why, Emma's as brown as a berry.'

'I can't think of a single brown kind of berry,' Mossy had said.

'Shush,' his mother whispered to him. She went on talking to Miss Silkin, and Mossy went on talking aloud to himself. 'Holly berry, no. Rose-hip berry, no. Mistletoe berry, of course not.'

'Will you, for goodness sake, be quiet,' Mother had said.

There weren't many berries on the common at this time of year, but he looked about him as they went. 'Juniper berries are blue,' he thought. 'Blackberries are black.' Miss Silkin was obviously wrong.

He heard a cuckoo calling out, somewhere ahead of them, in a wooded part of the common. It was his great longing to see a cuckoo and, instead of going towards the rubbish dump, as he had meant to do, he took another grassy path in the direction of the wood, listening carefully.

'I'm thirsty,' Emma said.

He put his finger to his lips, and went quietly on, leading her by the hand. It was cool – almost cold – inside the wood, with a mouldy smell. There were deep piles of black, rotten beech-leaves under the trees, and strange toadstools that Emma wanted to pick – and did grab up some. Mossy snatched them out of her hand, and made her rub her fingers on her dress, in case the toadstools were poisonous ones.

Then the cuckoo cried again, deeper in the wood, and high up, somewhere, among the top branches.

If I could only see it, Mossy thought.

'I'm cold,' Emma said.

'Another time, I won't bring you with me.'

She was not at all sure that she wanted him to; but she kept up with him bravely, hoping that the wood might soon end.

The cuckoo did not call out again. It had gone far ahead, or to roost. The path through the wood became narrower and narrower. Brambles looped across it, and scratched them, and sometimes Mossy had to lift Emma up and carry her over them. Beads of blood as big as holly berries came up on his legs. Now *he* was thirsty and cold, but he would hardly admit it to himself. He was a little bit nervous, too. He wondered if it were dark because they were in the wood, of if it were dark outside it, too; and getting late.

At last, the trees thinned, and they stepped out on to a wide, grassy glade, and he saw that it was not dark yet, but everything was sad-looking, and the sun had gone.

He looked quickly to right and left, not wanting Emma to see that he did not know which way to turn. They must surely be able to get home, he thought, without going back through the wood. He guessed that Emma would cry all the way if they had to, and he could not bear her tears, because they would be his fault.

As if he knew perfectly well just where they were going, he set off to the left. They turned a bend and there, at the edge of the wood, they saw an old man sitting by a little fire of twigs, toasting a piece of bacon on a fork. He was dressed in rags, with a cap pulled over his eyebrows, and he had a rough grey beard – not a kind-looking beard like Father Christmas's. He had built a shelter from branches and bracken, and was cooking his supper before lying down for the night.

When Mossy and Emma came near, he grinned at them, and his stumps of teeth were all black at the roots, so that his mouth when it was open looked like a worn-out old scrubbing-brush.

Mossy was frightened; but Emma seemed quite friendly to the old tramp. She liked the cosy look of his shelter and his fire, and the smell of scorched bacon, dripping fat into the flames.

'I'm hungry,' she said.

'No you're not,' Mossy said, quickly dragging her on.

'Like a nibble of bacon then, my duckie?' the old man shouted.

'I'm lost,' Emma wailed.

'We've got to hurry home to *our* supper,' Mossy said, trying to be polite but firm. He did not want to annoy the old man.

'You must never talk to people you don't know,' he said to Emma in a low voice.

59

'I like a nibble of bacon,' she shouted, looking backwards to the fire, as she was dragged on by her brother.

They could hear the old man laughing. He might be kind and harmless, Mossy thought, as he hurried Emma on; but it was better not to take risks, because they seemed to be far from home, and nobody knew where they were, least of all themselves.

When they were out of sight of the old man, he picked Emma up in his arms, and tried to hasten on with her; but she was too heavy, and soon he had to put her down. He stopped for a moment to listen; but, thank goodness, there was no sound of footsteps coming after them.

He began to feel as if they were two children in a fairy-tale. Perhaps if Emma *had* taken a nibble of bacon, the old man would have been changed suddenly into a Prince. Really, he did not believe this for one moment; but he had to keep thinking things to keep his mind busy.

'I'm hungry,' Emma said again.

'Would you eat some liver if you had it?' he could not help asking.

'No, I wouldn't,' she said furiously.

'You're not hungry, then,' he said.

'I know when I'm hungry. I'm going to eat some of those berries.'

Even in the gathering darkness, Mossy could see that

they were a shiny, bright red, and looked very danger-ous. 'No, you won't,' he said.

He knew that she was tired out, and that they would have to sit down and have a rest. He sank down on some soft grass and pulled her close to him. She whim-pered a little and snuggled up. Like the Babes in the Wood, he thought. But at least they *weren't* in the wood. The thought of it, and its awful blackness – worse by now – made him shudder.

He racked his brain for some help from all the desert-island books he had read, and had had read to him. But they seemed to be no help on a common, and at this time of the year – no fish, no birds' eggs; only berries, likely to be poisonous. If a goat came by, I could milk it, he thought. 'But what *into?*' Anyhow, no goat came by.

'Have some grass to eat,' he suggested to Emma. He pulled up a few blades and gave them to her. 'They're nice. Like salad, you know,' he explained.

'I don't like salad,' she cried, spitting out the grass, and rubbing her eyes with her fists. She yawned and yawned, and it was catching, and he began to yawn, too.

He stretched out his hand, and pulled the small flow-ers from some white nettles, and showed her how to suck the sweetness from the tips of them.

'It's honey,' he told her.

'I only like honey in pots, on my bread-and-butter,' she cried. 'I want some bread-and-butter.'

He thought, 'I just wouldn't be myself at this moment for all the tea in China.' Sometimes his mother said things like that – 'I wouldn't go through *that* again for all the tea in China.' It was when she was talking to people like Miss Silkin.

But he didn't want to think about his mother. She would be worried by now – long before this; and he hated her to be worried. And he longed for her so badly.

In some ways, having Emma with him made him braver. But in different ways it made him feel more fearful.

'Listen,' he said comfortingly to her. 'This is a very exciting adventure. It's like the Babes in the Wood.'

'I don't like being Babes in the Wood.'

It was certainly the wrong thing to have said, for at once she began to boo-hoo more loudly. 'There might be wolfs.'

'"Wolves",' he said, to correct her. But she thought he was just agreeing with her, and shrieked louder than ever.

There was a chestnut tree above them, and Mossy pulled off some leaves and tried to teach her how to make fishbones from them, by stripping out the green bits; but she was interested only for a second. He had a glimpse of what it must be like for Mother, having to keep her happy and amused all day, when he was at school, or out playing with his friends. He felt very old.

'I think we'd better go on a bit,' he said. 'Not long now.'

But as far as he could see, it might be all night. He had a blister on his heel and every step made it more sore.

It was dark, quite dark. The fallen leaves and bracken rustled, as if little creatures had begun to stir and move amongst them.

'I can hear wolfs,' Emma whispered.

'No, wolves make a noise like this,' Mossy explained, and he put back his head and howled so loud that she clung more tightly to his hand. He always seemed to do the wrong thing, meaning to do right.

Then, at the moment when he seemed to have lost all hope, a white shape floated down from the trees above them, making a clapping sound with its wings.

'It's an angel,' Emma said – as if she knew angels, and saw them every day.

But it was a big white owl. It glided on, swooped and disappeared, and then came back into sight again, just ahead of them.

The path they were on was joined by another path, and Mossy stopped, not knowing which one to take. There was nothing to make up his mind for him, but the fact of the owl hovering above, then floating on in one direction, as if it were leading the way.

It kept circling and swooping, vanishing then re-appearing, always just a little ahead and sometimes, when it was high on wing between the trees, it hooted myste-riously, and the sound echoed through the branches.

All at once, in front of them, Mossy saw little lights sweeping from side to side, and then heard voices call-ing, 'Emma! Mossy! Mossy! Emma!'

The voices were Father's and Selwyn's father's.

Mossy shouted out with all his might, and the voices answered them, and the flickering lights of the torches came nearer and nearer until they at last fell over Emma and Mossy and lit up the grasses at their feet.

'Where on *earth*?' Father began, in a tired, yet joyful voice. He had searched for them for hours, and longed to find them, and now that he had, he could not help being angry. 'Really, Mossy! You've worried your mother sick. We must hurry back, because she's in tears.'

He picked up Emma, and Selwyn's father, seeing how Mossy was limping, stooped down to give him a piggy-back.

'A grown-up *crying*!' Mossy said.

'No, it's all right, son. We'll soon cheer her up. But what on *earth* . . . ?'

'I was following a cuckoo,' Mossy tried to explain.

That seemed days ago, almost in another life. His relief was so wonderful, as he bumped uncomfortably along on Selwyn's father's back.

'But an owl brought us home,' he added.

'White owl,' Emma said, nearly asleep.

'The wise old owl,' said Selwyn's father, puffing badly, as he stumbled on. Mossy had one arm round his neck, and held the torch with his other hand, lighting up the uneven ground in front of them.

'Cuckoos are mischievous things,' Father said. 'They have no sense of responsibility.'

'I still like them,' Mossy said sleepily. 'I think I always shall. If only I could see one.'

The white owl, having seemed to guide them to safety, had flown away.

When they came near home, they could see Mother standing in the lighted window, staring out into the blackness of the common. Then she must have seen the lights of the torches, for she moved quickly from the window and the front door was opened wide, and she was *there*, and her arms were opened wide, too.

'No talk. Bed,' Father said, as they went into the house. 'You had a good adventure, like a story-book. We'll hear about it tomorrow.'

'But they can have some bread-and-milk first,' Mother said, and to Mossy the words 'bread-and-milk' seemed the most comforting ones in all the world.

They sat in the kitchen. Selwyn's father drank some whisky, and when the bread-and-milk was ready, Emma ate hers sitting on Mother's lap. There wasn't much left of it because of the baby coming.

Mossy was nearly asleep. He sprinkled some brown sugar into his bowl and ate slowly. It was so wonderful to be in the light and warm, and not out there, lost, on the cold common.

'There was an old man sitting by a fire . . . ' he began to tell them.

'Tomorrow,' Father said. 'We'll hear it all then.'

'You'll never go off again,' Mother said. 'Promise!'

'Laura!' Father said, frowning at Mother. He did not want the children to get over-excited by talking.

'Yes, I promise. I didn't mean to,' Mossy said.

'I wasn't frightened,' Emma said. 'Mossy took care of me. I wasn't at all frightened. I liked it. I liked it very much.'

She seemed to be waking up again, so Father picked her up gently, and carried her upstairs to bed.

Mossy looked across at his mother, and she smiled. It was a wavering, watery smile, as if perhaps she really had been crying. He could not understand that.

'It's very late,' she said softly. 'Up you go.'

6

Emma's Games and Mossy's Illness

The lovely summer was slipping by. There were the School Sports near the end of the term, and Mossy came second in the Sack Race, and won a jig-saw puzzle, which he would never have the patience to do; but he liked getting a prize.

Emma went into the Young Visitors' Race, but she did not win a prize. Even if her fat legs could ever have carried her fast enough, she did not give them a chance. She had a special little friend, who was a year younger than she. They met at the Clinic, where their mothers went about their coming babies, and they always played together there. Her name was Bunty, and when Emma was running along in the race, she looked round to see where Bunty was, and saw that she was a long way behind, so she stopped and waited for her to catch up, and then they went on together, hand-in-hand, towards the winning-post, although to them it was the losing post. Everyone laughed and clapped, and said, 'How charming!' But Mossy felt rather foolish, to think that his sister didn't know what a race was all about.

Then the school-holidays came – the long, summer-holidays, and there was the usual report – saying things like, 'Inattentive' and 'Could do better, if he cared to' and his father's usual disappointment.

Some of Mossy's friends went off to the sea-side. Octavius and all his older brothers and sisters went. Every year they stayed in a big, bare house by the sea, and Mossy thought what fun that must be.

Selwyn went camping with his parents. Other friends went off in caravans, or on boats, or to stay with their relations. The village seemed very empty. There was hardly ever anyone paddling round the edge of the village pond, or staring at the jars of sweets in the post office window.

Father had said they could not go away for a holiday this year, because they had had the expense of moving from London, and the baby was on the way and they would need to buy lots of things for him, or her, whichever it would be. To Mossy, this baby was becoming a bit of a bore.

Selwyn kindly sent a picture-postcard of a donkey.

When Mossy lifted up the saddle, a string of little folded photographs came out. They were views of the place where Selwyn was staying at that time.

Somehow, the card made Mossy feel lonelier than ever, and more than ever left out of exciting things.

He began to find it hard to pass the time. He was very careful about the common these days, and never strayed very far from home, although he still went to inspect the rubbish dump.

'What can I *do*? he kept asking his mother, although he knew that question made grown-ups lose their patience.

'Do?' she cried. 'Good heavens, my child, you've got a nice garden to play in. And a cupboard full of toys.'

'I wish I had a bicycle. Then I'd know what to do.'

'Well, you *haven't* got a bicycle,' she snapped. 'There are lots of things *I* haven't got that I'd like to have; but I don't make everyone's life a misery about them.'

'Well, I just don't know what to *do*.'

'You haven't touched that nice jig-saw puzzle you won at the Sports.'

'I don't care about that old thing. I wish I'd won a kite like Selwyn did.'

Mossy was in a thoroughly bad mood.

'Well, *I* wish you'd go out of this kitchen, and not be under my feet all the time.'

Mother seemed in a thoroughly bad mood, too. She

took up a fork and pressed it all round the edges of a pie to make a pattern, then she opened the oven door and let out a puff of heat.

Emma was kneeling up at the table, with one of Mother's aprons tied round her neck and her sleeves pushed up. She was cutting out shapes with some left-over scraps of pastry. She kept thumping them with her fist, and the pastry was grey with dirt. 'It's for Daddy's tea,' she said.

'He won't eat that rubbish,' Mossy said.

'He will so,' said Emma calmly. She pressed her elbow on a piece to flatten it, and was pleased when the pattern of stitches of her knitted jersey was printed on it. She thought she had hit on a new idea in cooking, and showed them proudly.

'Very pretty,' Mother said, hardly glancing at it, she was so busy. Because her hands were floury, she had to blow a wisp of hair out of her eyes. She always had a very red face when she was baking.

'You never give *me* any pastry,' Mossy grumbled.

'Don't be so babyish,' was all she said.

'It *might* be for my children's tea,' Emma said, wondering if she could spare anything so beautiful for anyone to really eat. 'It's called a knitted pie,' she went on. 'My children love knitted pie.'

She had an imaginary family – a large family of boys and girls (not *many* boys, and only baby ones), and cats and dogs. She had just bought an imaginary pony, too, and she was quite content with it. Mossy knew he could never be contented with an imaginary bicycle.

He went off to look at the rubbish dump, but there was nothing new there. The common was hot, and quiet – except for birds twittering. The cuckoo had flown away weeks ago, and Mossy had not managed to get a glimpse of it. He wandered about amongst the bracken, but not very far from home.

When he got back, the pie was out of the oven and stood on the kitchen table, golden-brown and steaming. There were some jam-tarts, too; because Emma's friend, Bunty, and her mother were coming to tea. Emma's pastry-shapes were on the table, too – all covered with burnt currants.

Father was at home every day now because of the school-holidays, and he mowed the lawn, and did jobs about the house, such as putting up shelves and painting Emma's old cot in readiness for the new baby. This quite excited her, so that *she* thought she would have a new baby, too. 'And a donkey,' she added. 'I shall call the donkey Poor Old Gertie.'

'That wouldn't be very sensible,' Mother said; but Mossy saw that she had to go and stand in the larder for a moment or two, until she had stopped laughing.

When Bunty came to tea, Emma told her, 'I've just

had another little girl. Her name is Shaky,' she said, because it was the first word that came into her head.

Bunty seemed quite excited, too. She played Emma's games obediently, and took any part that she was given. Sometimes, she was Emma's husband, or the nurse-maid, and other times she had to be one of the children, and lie curled up in the cardboard box the groceries had come in. And she would suck her thumb and make baby-noises, until Mossy was disgusted.

This afternoon she was in the cardboard box, making out she had measles; and Emma was standing on tiptoe by a hollyhock, pretending it was a telephone. 'Hello! Goodbye!' she kept saying into the flower.

'Fancy talking to a hollyhock,' Mossy said.

She turned quickly and frowned. 'I'm ringing up the doctor,' she explained.

'Mossy!' Mother said warningly. 'Let them play. They're being so good.' Her voice sounded as if she would add, 'Not like you.'

The two mothers sat in deck-chairs, knitting, and talking about names for their next babies. Bunty's mother hoped for a boy; but Mossy's mother, already having one of each, did not mind at all.

'Venetia's a pretty name.'

'Oh, *so* pretty,' Mother agreed.

'I like quite plain names for a boy, though, like George.'

'Yes, George is awfully nice.'

Father, who was gardening nearby, moved farther off. He had had this sort of conversation many times before. Sometimes, when he and Mother were in bed, and he was as good as off to sleep, Mother would wake him up, and ask, 'What do you think of Harriet, or Catherine?'

'Very nice. Have both,' he'd mumble. And then drop off to sleep again.

'Or, if it's a boy, perhaps Thomas would be nice.'

And then he simply could not rouse himself to reply. He often wondered if she went on talking to herself for half the night.

'Mossy, you be the doctor,' Emma called out.

'No fear.'

'But my little darling's got measles, and I can't find any doctor.'

'Too bad,' he said. He hated Emma's games.

'You're a very, very cruel boy,' she said, stamping her foot.

Bunty, curled up in the cardboard box, cried louder than ever.

'Give me a hand with this honeysuckle,' Father said to Mossy, coming to his rescue and holding out a piece of string.

'I hope the next baby will be a boy,' Mossy said in a low voice, as they tied back the honeysuckle. 'We've got too many girls.' As there was only one, this was rather rude; but Father smiled.

All the time they were having tea on the lawn, Emma went on and on talking in her bossy, mother's voice to Bunty, who still had to be a baby even when she was eating a jam-tart.

Mossy could not eat *his* jam-tart. He took one little bite, and then put the tart back on his plate, as if he could not bear the sight of it. His throat hurt, and he felt hot.

'What's the matter, old chap?' his father asked.

'I'm hot.'

His mother glanced at him quickly. 'Oh, dear,' she said. 'You certainly do look a bit flushed.'

She got up and put her hand anxiously on Mossy's forehead.

'It's my throat hurting,' Mossy said.

'I think you'd be better off in bed.'

He thought of cool sheets, and the curtains drawn so that the room would be dim and restful. He put his plate down on the grass and got up. This made his mother more anxious than ever. It was quite unlike Mossy to go up to bed without making a fuss.

'I'll take him up,' Father said, and they went indoors together, he and Mossy. He put his arm round Mossy's shoulders.

'I do hope it's nothing infectious,' Mother said, looking at Bunty.

'Oh, don't worry about that,' Bunty's mother said, with a sort of tinny cheerfulness, and then, in a more natural voice, she added, 'After all, they haven't been *very near* to one another.'

Upstairs, it was at first just as Mossy had imagined it would be. The sheets were cool and smooth, and he lay very still and watched the drawn curtains for their slightest movement. But there was hardly any breeze.

Presently, he heard Bunty and her mother saying goodbye.

'Bye, bye, tiny baby,' Emma shouted. She had really tired Mossy out that day with her chatter. When he felt well, he hardly noticed it.

'I hope he'll feel better in the morning,' Bunty's mother said.

Now it was quieter down in the garden, although Emma was talking on the hollyhock telephone again.

Soon Mother came up, and put the thermometer in Mossy's mouth. While he was lying there, with his mouth carefully closed, she went quietly about the room, tidying up, putting his clothes away, blowing some dust off the top of the chest-of-drawers. Mossy knew that this meant she expected to have to call in the doctor. He wondered if doctors ever saw bedrooms as they usually are – so much straightening-up goes on before their visits. It must give them a very untrue picture of people's homes.

Mother took the thermometer from his mouth and went to the window to peer at it. Then she shook it, and said cheerfully, 'Well, there's nothing much to worry about *there*.' But she went on tidying up the room, so the thought of the doctor was obviously still in her mind.

'I'm *so* hot!' Mossy complained, for the once cool, smooth sheets were warm and crumpled now.

'Say "Ah!"' Mother told him, and she looked down his throat. 'O.K. I'll straighten your bed and bring you some lemonade.'

The lemonade was in a glass jug. It had slices of lemon floating in it and ice-cubes jostling and clinking with a beautiful cool sound. He drank some and felt better.

'Would you like me to read to you?' she asked.

He nodded. It hurt him to speak.

'What shall we have?'

He shut his eyes, and said, 'Tom Kitten.' He was afraid she would say it was too babyish, but, instead, she said, 'Oh, lovely!' and went off to Emma's bedroom to fetch it.

He just wanted, at this moment, a book whose words he knew all by heart. He did not feel up to anything new.

When the book was read – so quickly – Mother had to put Emma to bed.

In the summer, there were what grown-ups called 'the short nights'. Mossy could never understand this. To him, they had always seemed nearly endless, lying there while it was still light, tossing and turning, and scratching gnat-bites.

This evening, too, seemed dreadfully long. He could hear his father going round the garden, watering the plants.

'It's so sultry,' Mother's voice said, floating up. 'It feels thundery to me.'

A delicious smell of wet garden came into the bedroom, and then Mossy heard the swish-swish of water against the wall below his window. Father was hosing the hot bricks, which had stored up the day's sun, and a coolness began to come off them. There was the sound of dripping leaves, as the water spattered on a climbing rose.

'That should cool the house down,' said Father. He sounded in good spirits. Like Mossy, he loved playing with water. 'If it rains *now*, I'll be mad,' he said.

But it *did* rain. In the night, lightning forked across the sky, and thunder broke over the house. It was like being under a railway-bridge, with an express train going over. All the rest of the night it rained, steadily and heavily, beating against the dry earth.

No one knew then; but it was the end of that lovely, hot summer. The sunshine never really came back again, only for a peep through clouds.

I'll bet Selwyn gets washed out of his tent, Mossy thought, lying awake, listening to the storm. Although he knew it was mean of him, he could not make himself be sorry. He enjoyed imagining it.

The next morning, it was so much cooler that it was surprising to Mossy that his forehead was still burning. His hands and feet, though, were like ice.

His mother washed him and changed his pyjamas and combed his hair, which always stuck up like feathers on the top of his head. Then she said that Doctor Primrose was calling in that morning after his Surgery.

Doctor Primrose was quite nice, although he was rather shy, especially with children, and he didn't say much. He had thin sandy hair and he wore half-moon spectacles and looked over the tops of them. He held Mossy's tongue down with a spoon and shone a torch into his mouth.

'It's those tonsils again,' he said to Mother.

Sometimes, before this Mossy had felt ill in exactly the same way. Mother would tell people, 'Mossy's got one of his throats' – as if he had more than one, and could choose which he would have each day, as Emma chose her hair-ribbons.

'I think we'll have to deal with them,' the doctor said. 'But I'd rather leave it for a week or two.'

He went to wash his hands in the bathroom, and

Mossy was sure that that had been tidied up, too. It never was in the ordinary way.

When he had gone, Mother came back into the bedroom.

'What did he mean "deal with them"?' Mossy asked.

'Well, some time later on, he thinks it would be better to have your tonsils out. They're such a nuisance to you. And then you won't be ill any more.'

'Have them *out?*' Mossy tried to shout – but trying hurt him.

'My dear boy, it's just like having a bad tooth taken out, that's been making you feel wretched all the time.'

'But my throat's much better today. Tomorrow it will be quite better.'

'You'll keep on having these attacks. It's only sensible to get rid of the trouble.'

'Will it be in hospital?'

'Yes – for a day or two. They will give you something to make you go to sleep, and when you wake up, hey presto! the horrid tonsils will have gone for ever. And then they'll give you some ice-cream to eat.'

'Yes, I know.' He remembered a boy at school telling him.

'It's nothing to worry about.'

'When will it be?'

'Doctor Primrose will tell us. He knows best.'

A rather nice thought suddenly came to Mossy.

'Mother,' he said. 'I shan't be better in time for the wedding, shall I?'

'But, of course, my darling,' she said cheerfully. 'You mustn't worry about *that*. You'll be as fit as a fiddle by then.'

Oh, dear! No good, he thought. Now he had two nasty things looming ahead – hospital and the wedding – and he could not make up his mind which was the worst.

Apart from his sore throat and not being able to swallow much, he had rather a nice day. Father came up and read to him, and peeled grapes for him. And he had jelly and orange juice. He was made a great fuss of.

In the afternoon, Mother brought in a cardboard box-lid. She had made a forest in it, with leafy twigs stuck into plasticine, and he sat up in bed and made little plasticine animals, and put them under the trees. When he was tired, he lay back against the pillows, and half shut his eyes, and imagined the wild beasts roaming about under the branches – wolves and tigers and reindeer: thin plasticine snakes curled round the trunks of the trees. And he talked softly to himself, explaining about the animals and what they were doing.

So much was pleasant about being ill – if only he had felt well, then he could have enjoyed it more.

7

Alison

The summer was now quite over. The cherry-trees dropped their thin yellow leaves on to the grass, and the autumn flowers were out in the garden – Michaelmas daisies and golden-rod. Big striped spiders spun beautiful webs from stem to stem, and the hedges on the damp, misty mornings were covered with cobwebs.

The common was beginning to change colour, and soon would be red and gold, with conkers and beech-nuts falling. A good time of the year coming up, Mossy thought. His throat was quite better now, and he had forgotten about being ill.

He set off for the first day of the term, wearing his new winter clothes – stiff new shoes, scratchy new socks and a new raincoat which was too long in the sleeves, too long altogether; but he was growing fast, his mother said.

After the first novelty had worn off, school seemed as dull as ever, and he began to fidget, and to whisper to Octavius who sat next to him. Then he got hiccups, which made everyone except Miss Blackett giggle. Even after the hiccups had stopped he pretended they were going on, and made louder and louder noises, until Miss Blackett lost her patience, which she did not like doing on the very first morning of the term. She made him go up to the front of the class and sit there under her nose, until he could stop showing-off. The hiccups ceased immediately.

All the girls suddenly had a craze for skipping; but the boys felt they had nothing very much to do until the conker season started up.

The first week of the term dragged and then, on Friday, Mother said that the next day Miss Silkin was bringing Alison to tea.

'Who's Alison?' Mossy asked suspiciously.

'She's Miss Silkin's little niece. She lives in London. We've already told you about her. She's going to be a bridesmaid at the wedding. The two of you are to hold the train. So Miss Silkin thought it would be nice for you to meet.'

'Hold what train?' Mossy asked, puzzled.

'It's a sort of – well, it's a long piece of her dress that you hold up for her,' Mother tried to explain.

Mossy could not picture this. The very idea would have made him laugh, if he had not felt so depressed.

That wedding! With the colder weather, it was coming nearer. This was a certainty, unless Miss Silkin's future husband backed out at the last moment. Fortunately, however, nothing more had been said about his tonsils and the hospital. That might have been forgotten.

'Mother!' he said, in a low, troubled voice. He was hardly able to say what was in his mind. He paused.

'Yes, Mossy?' she replied. She was sitting by the fire, sewing. She was always doing something. She bit off a piece of cotton, and looked up at him.

'Mother!' he said again, desperately. He licked his lips, and then asked, in a rush, 'What have I got to wear?'

'When, darling?'

'At the wedding.' He stared down at the rug, and grew very red in the face.

'Ah, the wedding. You'll be wearing the kilt.'

'A *kilt?*'

'Yes, the Robertson tartan. I was a Robertson before I was married, you see,' she said proudly. 'So it is perfectly right for you to wear it.'

'Oh, *thank you*, Mother,' he said.

'What for?'

'For being a Robertson before you were married.'

He thought that if it hadn't been for that, he might have had to wear velvet trousers, or something terrible and babyish of the kind. He thanked his lucky stars for having a Scottish mother. He did not in the least mind wearing a kilt. He would not even mind Selwyn seeing him wearing it. He would rather have liked him to.

'I wish I had asked you before,' he said.

She looked up and smiled. 'Yes, it's always best to ask if you're worried about anything. Other people can't guess what's going on in your head. You might be worrying for nothing.'

He had been.

Although the kilt was something to be relieved about, the visit of Miss Silkin and her niece was a different matter.

The next afternoon, he went down to the village post office to spend his pocket-money.

'Don't be long,' his mother called after him. 'Miss Silkin will be here at four o'clock and it will be nice for Alison to have someone to play with.'

He went off down the cart-track feeling scornful. A grown-up should know that a boy of his age didn't *play*. He *did* things, he *discovered* things, he turned things into different things; but he did not play. 'Can Bunty come to play?' Emma would ask. And that was all right at her age.

At the post office he met Octavius. They both bought lollies and comics and went and sat in the bus-shelter by the pond, and turned pages peacefully, and Mossy licked his lolly, and said nothing. He preferred being with boys.

'Aren't you going to eat your lolly?' he asked Octavius.

'No, I'm waiting till you haven't got one,' Octavius explained.

'I suppose I'd better go,' Mossy said after a while. 'A girl is coming to tea.'

'Bad luck,' said Octavius, reading on.

'Want to swop comics?' Mossy asked.

'No, thanks, I've read that already.'

'O.K. *Be* like that.'

'I said I've read it.'

'I heard you.'

It was obvious that Octavius was in one of his nasty moods.

He folded his own comic, stuffed it into his pocket, and walked sadly homewards. He had no idea of the time.

There was a clock in the butcher's shop, and he squinted in through the window, and saw to his horror that it was nearly half-past four. The butcher came out of the shop to tell him not to breathe on the glass, but he was round the bend of the road by then, and running as fast as his legs would carry him.

He was quite breathless when he reached home, and he hoped his mother would be cross with him in private, not in front of a strange girl.

As he went down the path, he could hear a

commotion coming from inside the house. Someone else seemed to be getting into trouble.

'I told you not to.' It was Miss Silkin's voice. 'That's what comes of disobedience.'

Mossy felt very curious. He went in through the kitchen door, and made his way quietly to the sitting-room.

'Your new dress!' Miss Silkin was saying. 'And your tights! Just look at those new tights.'

Mother said, in a softer, kinder voice than Miss Silkin's, 'Well, I don't think there are any bones broken. That's all that really matters. Ah, there you are, Mossy, at last. I'm afraid poor Alison's had a bit of an accident.'

The tea was ready on the trolley, but had not been started yet. Alison was lying on the sofa, and Mother was bathing a cut on her forehead. The room smelt of disinfectant.

'I'm sorry,' the girl said, looking at Mossy. 'I'm afraid I broke your tree-house.'

'I always thought it unsafe,' Miss Silkin said to Mother. 'I was surprised that you and Robert permitted it.'

'It was my own fault. I'm very sorry,' Alison said again to Mossy. 'My foot slipped, and I came crashing down, and some of the tree-house came with me.'

'It doesn't matter,' he said.

He was so surprised to think of a girl climbing a tree, that he could not think of anything else to say.

'Ouch!' she cried, as Mother dabbed her forehead with some cotton-wool.

'Now try not to be a baby,' her Aunt Vera – Miss Silkin – said.

'Babies don't climb trees,' said Mossy.

When Mother had finished bathing Alison's forehead, she took the bowl of water and the towel out to the kitchen.

'I'll make the tea for you,' said Miss Silkin, following, and Emma trotted after them. Mossy and Alison were left alone. He stared at her. She had carroty-red hair in pigtails, and she was at the age when she had lost two of her top front teeth. Her face was pale and covered with freckles. She wore a torn, dark blue dress, and green tights which were torn, too. She looked fagged-out, but grinned bravely.

'They told me I mustn't climb the tree; but I couldn't help it,' she said.

Mossy understood.

'We haven't any trees in our garden in London.'

'I know. I used to live in London,' he said.

'I'd rather live here,' Alison said. 'I do wish I lived here.'

'There's a nice rubbish dump on the common.'

He suddenly felt he wanted to tell her everything,
show her everything.

'We got lost on the common – me and Emma,' he
said. 'We were out there when it was quite dark. There
was an old tramp who'd lit a fire, but I wouldn't let
Emma talk to him.'

'I wish I'd been there.'

'I wish you had been, too.'

'Were you scared?'

He hesitated; then he felt that she was the first person he had ever been able to speak the truth to – the whole truth.

'I was pretty scared,' he said.

'I'd have been scared, too,' she said. 'All the same, I wish I'd been there.'

She waved her hand in the direction of the cake on the trolley.

'I know that seedy cake of old,' she said. 'My mother makes it every time Aunt Vera comes to tea. I hate it. Sorry to be rude.'

'I hate it, too.'

'What are they making you wear for the wedding?' Mossy asked her.

'Some fool old thing. I dread it. And I dreaded you, till now.'

She's not pretty, he thought. It's worse for her. They'll make her wear pretty clothes, and she'll hate it.

'Emma actually *wants* to be a bridesmaid,' he said.

'Well, I'll stand down. With pleasure.'

'No, don't stand down,' he said, feeling quite alarmed at the idea.

'Ouch!' she said again, shifting her legs. 'I'll be in such trouble when I get home. I've torn all of my new clothes. Is your mother strict?'

'On and off,' said Mossy.

'Mine's a holy terror. When I spill things on the tablecloth, I have to cover the whole stain with pennies. That's to pay for the laundry. The bigger the stain, the more it costs me. Bang goes my pocket-money. What do you think of *that* for a punishment?'

'For pity's sake don't tell my mother about it,' Mossy begged her. 'She's got enough ideas already.'

'Do you take me for an idiot?' Alison asked.

He certainly did not.

The others returned, and tea began. Miss Silkin, of course, was telling Mother about the wedding plans – about the three-tiered cake and her bouquet, and what hymns they would have, and which wedding-march.

Mossy thought:

> *Here comes the bride,*
> *All fat and wide.*

He wished that he could have said this aloud to make Alison laugh. But it really could not describe Miss Silkin, who was tall and thin.

Although they had known one another for only a few minutes, Mossy and Alison already had some private jokes. For instance, when Mossy spilt some milk, Alison looked steadily up at the ceiling, saying nothing, but making a funny face. And when Mother offered her some seed cake, she said politely, 'I think I would rather have a biscuit.' She leaned forward and took one, and rolled her eyes at Mossy, who began to giggle.

Mother thought he was behaving stupidly, but was relieved that the two seemed to be getting on so well. It would make things easier at the wedding.

When Miss Silkin said that it was time for them to go, Alison limped stiffly down the path and got into the car.

'See you in church,' she shouted to Mossy.

It was so strange. He had begun to look forward to the wedding more than he had ever looked forward to anything in his life.

8

In Hospital

'When you have the baby, will you go to the hospital?'
Mossy asked his mother. He vaguely remembered hearing that this had happened when Emma was born. It
had been a dull time for him, because Miss Silkin had
come to look after him.

Mother said, 'Yes.'

'Then what about us?' he asked, hoping that it would
not be the same thing again.

Luckily, it seemed that Miss Silkin now had other
things to take up her time.

'You are going to Selwyn's during the day,' Mother
explained. 'You can stay there, and Father will fetch
Emma when he comes home from work.'

This was quite cheering news. He liked Selwyn's
mother. She was square-shaped and cosy, like Mrs

Noah. He and Selwyn would sleep in the same room, and lie awake and talk all night, and Mrs Noah would tap on the wall between her bedroom and theirs, and for a while they would whisper, and then forget to whisper, and the tapping would begin again. All this had happened before when, for some reason, he had gone to stay there.

He would look forward to it. Mother said she was looking forward to it, too; because she wanted the baby so much, and was tired of wearing the same old clothes. When she was not fat any longer, she said, she was going to buy a new dress. She seemed to be thinking about, and longing for, this new dress, as Mossy thought about, and longed for, a bicycle.

Then, suddenly, it was not Mother going to hospital they talked about, but Mossy's going there himself – quite soon, to have his tonsils out.

Doctor Primrose came one day, and said, 'Well I think we can see to that little matter next week,' and Mossy's stomach seemed to roll over, he felt so scared, now that it was really going to happen.

Children at school told him it was nothing, but he knew that he would have to find out for himself.

Mother bought him some new pyjamas, and let down his dressing-gown, because he was growing out of it. (She was always complaining that he was growing too fast – as if it were somebody's fault. He wondered if she would like him to be a midget to make things less trouble for her.)

His case was packed, and he put in his bird book and his shabby old copy of *Charlotte's Web*. He also put in his water-pistol, but Mother took it out again, saying that a hospital was not a suitable place for it. Indeed, as far as she was concerned, she could not think of *any* suitable place for it. There had been a lot of trouble about it, from time to time, and it was usually on a high shelf, out of reach, confiscated.

When the day for hospital came, it seemed a different kind of day from any he had ever known. 'It's really here,' he kept telling himself – as he always did on Christmas Day; but *then* he did so with a happy amazement; not feeling sick, as now.

When Father came home from school, rather earlier than usual, he took Mossy to the hospital in the car. Mother and Emma came too, and Emma seemed quite excited, as if they were all going off on a holiday, or something very nice of that kind.

It was a sad time of day, Mossy thought, as they drove through the village. Selwyn was outside the post office and, as they went by, he did a thumb-up sign to Mossy, looking very serious and impressed for once, so that Mossy suddenly felt heroic and important. He did the thumb-up sign back – like hitch-hikers trying to get a lift – but they did not smile at one another.

The hospital was built on the hill outside the nearest town – the town where Father's school was. It was a big red building with gardens round it.

'I'll take you in, Mossy,' Father said, getting out of the car.

'I'll come tomorrow,' Mother promised, kissing him. 'And I'll bring you a little present.'

Emma was still bouncing about, full of glee.

The hospital had a strange smell – neither nice nor nasty: just very strange. It was a mixture of disinfectant and floor-polish and cooking. Not a homely smell.

Mossy and his father walked along a wide, slippery passage, Father carrying the little case, as if Mossy were already too ill to do so. A nurse took them to the Children's Ward. There were rows of beds, and some cots.

Father said, 'You'll be all right, old chap,' and then he said 'Goodbye', and was gone.

The nurse helped Mossy to undress and get into his bed – a thing he could perfectly well have done for himself.

On one side of him was a very young child – younger than Emma – sitting up in a cot, grizzling; and, on the other side, was a West Indian boy of about Mossy's age, with a dark brown face and short curly hair. He stared at Mossy, as if he were wondering what he was going to be like – friend or foe.

On the walls all round the room were babyish pictures of rabbits and fairies, and elves sitting on toadstools.

The nurse put Mossy's books and washing things into a cupboard beside his bed. Soon, feeling rather shy because of all the staring eyes, Mossy leaned over and took out his bird book and, keeping his head down, began to turn the pages.

'My name is Stephen,' said the boy in the next bed, after a while.

Mossy looked up, thankful to have been spoken to at last. 'Mine's Mossy,' he said.

'Tomorrow, I'm going to have my adenoids taken out,' Stephen said. 'Then I shan't be so silly.'

Mossy thought he seemed quite sensible as he was. He just had a rather sing-song, snuffly voice, as if his head were bunged up and he could not breathe and talk at the same time.

'My Mam says I act silly,' the boy went on. 'When I get my adenoids out, I shan't act silly any more, she says.'

Mossy could think of quite a few people who might be improved in this way.

They talked about their illnesses for a time, and then about other things.

The small child next to Mossy kept crying from temper, and throwing things over the side of the cot.

'Shut up,' said Mossy sternly.

'Yeah, you shut up,' Stephen added.

They agreed about things, and were friends.

Sometimes, in the night, Mossy woke up. It was all so strange, and each time he woke it took him a little while to remember where he was. Here, it was not dead quiet as it was at home in the middle of the night. There were little rustling sounds of children turning over in bed, and puffing, sometimes snoring, breathing noises.

All was quiet from the cot next to him: in fact, there had been very little trouble after he and Stephen had taken a firm line. It had worked better than any firm line he had ever tried to take with Emma.

When morning came, Stephen went off first to the operating-theatre. The nurse dressed him in a special white nightgown, and he was lifted on to a trolley and wheeled away. He grinned rather sleepily at Mossy, and Mossy decided that *he* would grin when his turn came. He hated waiting for it, though. He felt sick, as if his stomach were full of curdled milk.

It was not very long before Stephen was wheeled back again. He was fast asleep. It was just as Mossy's mother had said it would be.

'O.K., Sunny Jim!' the nurse said briskly to Mossy, wheeling the trolley to his bed. He did not care to be called 'Sunny Jim', but guessed that she only meant to be friendly. He wished that Selwyn and Octavius and Mother and Father could see how bravely, cheerfully he went out of the ward and along a passage towards the operating-theatre. But most especially, he would have liked Alison to know. Perhaps the nurse would tell his mother, who would tell Miss Silkin, and it would get round to Alison in that way. It was worth trying, and in some mysterious way, the trying made him feel better himself, even if no one else was ever to know. In any case, he felt quite calm and drowsy, from a prick they had given him in his arm.

Going along the passage was the last thing he could remember afterwards, seeing the tops of trees through the windows, and hearing the crackle of the nurse's apron.

He had often heard about 'coming round' – as it was called – after operations; but all that happened to him was that he opened his eyes and saw the dazzling white apron of a nurse who was standing by his bed. It was too bright, like sunlight on crisp snow, and he shut his eyes again, and went back to sleep.

When he woke up again, he found that his throat was sore, and there was a nasty taste in his mouth. But it was all over. He felt peaceful and relieved.

He was drowsy for most of the day. Even when

Mother came, he could scarcely rouse himself. She sat by his bed, and he was glad to know that she was there but, afterwards, he could not remember much about her visit. She had put a little parcel into his hand before she left and he had smiled and nodded; but it was some time before he could bother to open it. One of the nurses helped him.

It was a model of a car. It was a model of the very car Grandfather had, and which Mossy had always admired so much. Even the boot lifted up, and had tiny suitcases inside.

'It's cute,' the nurse said.

It was the last thing it was.

Languidly, he handed it across to Stephen.

'Man, it's a fine car,' Stephen said.

And Mossy nodded.

If Stephen had ever acted silly, which Mossy did not for a moment believe, he was not acting silly now. Tomorrow, he would tell him about Grandfather – about his car, and Fortnum, and Poor Old Gertie, and that dreadful outing with the ginger-beer.

Next day, the ice-cream began in earnest, and it was the only thing he could take comfortably – even a drink went down with painful gulps.

In the afternoon, Mother came again and, this time, he could sit up and enjoy having her there. She had brought Emma with her, but other children were not allowed into the ward in case they brought germs; so she was left to play in the garden which Mossy could see through the window between his and Stephen's beds. She was dancing round a tree, playing one of her games. Mossy could see her lips moving.

'It's not to be opened until I've gone,' Mother said, putting a package on his locker. 'But it's only a very small present this time. Emma thinks I am spoiling you. She said such an amusing thing when I was wrapping it up. "What a way to bring up children," she said, in a very grown-up voice. I can't think where she gets all these things from.'

Mossy knew, but didn't say.

'It's those games she plays. She lives in her own little world.'

'You mustn't sit on my bed,' he whispered to her. 'It's not allowed.'

She got off obediently.

It seemed strange to be telling her not to do things. It was usually the other way about.

He looked out of the window again, and saw Emma standing under a tree, wagging her finger crossly at some imaginary child.

'She's nuts,' he said.

Stephen's mother was also visiting. She had the same dark face and frizzy hair as Stephen's, and the same wide grin; but she was enormously fat, and the fat swayed as she walked, and her face wobbled when she laughed. She was reading aloud from some comics she had brought, and Stephen lay back on his pillows and listened intently. Her voice was very deep, but her laugh was a surprisingly high chuckle.

'Would you like me to read to *you*?' Mossy's mother asked.

He shook his head. 'No, just tell me everything that's happened at home, while I've been away.'

'Well, there hasn't been time for anything much to happen. Not quite two days yet.'

'Tell me what you had to eat.'

While his mother was trying to remember every bite they had had, he put his hand out, and fidgeted with the string of the parcel she had brought. Without a word, she moved it out of his reach. He certainly did not want her to go home yet but, on the other hand, he was impatient to tear open the package.

Now he could see Emma picking some late daisies off the lawn. Then, to his horror, she went to one of the flower-beds and snapped off some golden-rod. He knocked on the window and, when she looked up, he shook his head sternly. He had to stay in this place, and he did not want to be in trouble because of *her*.

'It's very naughty to bang on the windows,' said his unfavourite nurse, who happened to be going down the ward at that moment. And Mother blushed, as she always did when other people told off a child of hers. She felt that it was *her* place to do that, and she also felt that she was being blamed for not doing so.

Then a bell rang, and it was time for all the visitors to go. The mothers got up, and kissed their children, and smiled and smiled, as if leaving them were the gayest thing in the world. Some of them looked quite tearful, in spite of their smiles.

Some of the children – especially the one in the cot next to Mossy – began to howl, and Mossy hoped his mother wouldn't be hurt if he did not join in.

'Try to cheer up that little one,' she whispered. 'He's really only a baby.'

As soon as all the visitors had gone, most of the crying stopped, and Mossy snatched up his parcel and opened it. Inside was a puzzle with a glass lid. There were little silver balls rolling about, and he was supposed to get them all into some holes. As fast as he got them in, they came out again. He thought he would go mad.

Then he remembered that he had not waved good-bye to Emma. He leaned over and looked out of the window, but the garden was empty now. Mother and Emma had gone, and so had all the daisies.

'Here we are then, tin-ribs,' said one of the nurses, bringing him some more ice-cream.

Nurses certainly had some peculiar names for him – tin-ribs, sober-sides, poppet, and Sunny Jim. Whatever next?

This time there were two kinds of ice-cream – strawberry and vanilla.

He ate the pink first, because it was his favourite. He never saved a nice thing till last. He might have lost his appetite before he came to it. Or it might have melted. He ate so slowly now, with his sore throat. In fact, his throat was sorer now than it had ever been. He had told his mother this, and asked where was the sense of coming to hospital to be made worse, but she had explained that this was a passing thing, and that in a day or two he would be better than he had ever been.

She and Emma would be on the bus now, going home to tea in the kitchen. They were two different worlds – home and hospital – and he was glad now that he knew about both.

9

One Lie After Another

'Well, it seems that that boy of mine behaved himself well in hospital,' Father boasted one evening to Selwyn's father, who had dropped in.

'So did that boy of *mine*,' Mother said, half-laughing and half-snappy.

She sometimes said that it seemed that Mossy was only hers when he was naughty. Then Father would say, of course, 'Just see what that boy of yours has done now,' meaning a broken window, or some damage from the water-pistol, or a nasty remark on a school-report.

Mossy had been home from hospital a day or two, but he was in bed when Selwyn's father came round with some bad news.

Mother's baby was expected at any time now, and Selwyn had gone down with mumps.

'I'm very sorry,' Selwyn's father kept saying – as if it were all his fault.

Now it would be impossible for Mossy and Emma to go to Mrs Noah's all day, while Mother was in hospital and Father at work.

'No fault of yours, dear fellow,' Father said.

Mother tried not to look worried; but, as soon as Selwyn's father had gone, she stopped trying, and said, 'What on earth can we do?'

'We'll think of something,' Father said, to comfort her. 'Someone will come to the rescue.'

In the end, it was the most surprising person who *did* come to the rescue, the last person anyone would ever have thought of.

When Mossy was quite better, he went back to school again. He was rather fed up with everything at present. He had lost all that importance he had had in hospital, and now that he was back to normal, everything seemed very flat. He was naughty and peevish. It was reaction, Doctor Primrose said – but Mossy neither knew nor cared what 'reaction' meant. Mother said he was just playing up, after being spoilt too much.

Whatever he did, small mistakes seemed to lead him into bigger ones. He got into great muddles when he did not mean to – as he did on the dreadful day of the odd shoes.

He was running to school that morning because he was late. He had not got out of bed when he was told, and had had to bolt his breakfast, as Mother called it, and he had a stomach-ache.

When he had nearly reached school, he stopped running for a moment because he was puffed, and then it was that he glanced down, and saw that he was wearing odd shoes – one black, with a leather sole, and one brown, with a rubber one.

It was too late to go back home and change them. He got into prayers only by the skin of his teeth and while

they were singing a hymn, he realized that some of the girls were giggling and nudging one another and looking at his feet. There was a little gang of them – Nancy and Jane and Elizabeth-Anne in particular – who, by their silly behaviour, had completely turned him against all girls. That was, until he had met Alison.

The whole school gathered together for prayers in a big room, and when he went back to his own classroom, he began to limp badly and look pained. He thought this quite a good idea of his.

'What's up?' Octavius asked.

'I've got a bad foot,' Mossy explained. 'That's why I have to wear this odd shoe. I couldn't get the other one on.'

'Bad luck,' said Octavius, obviously not interested.

Miss Blackett, however, seemed *very* interested, *too* interested for Mossy's liking.

'How did you manage to do that?' she asked him.

'I got it caught in a rabbit-trap,' he said. 'On the common.'

As he was being forced into telling one lie after another, he thought they might as well be interesting ones.

'Well, you *are* in the wars lately,' she said.

He admitted he was, and tried to look fagged-out.

At break, Miss Blackett insisted that he should stay in the classroom and drink his milk and rest his foot.

The others were racing and shrieking in the playground and having a fine old time. He decided that by tomorrow his foot should have made a perfect recovery. He also decided that he would never get into this sort of fix again.

All day long at school he limped about, trying not to forget to, and trying to remember which foot was hurting. The *brown* one is bad, he had to keep reminding himself. After a time, he had so got into the habit that he felt it would be surprising if he ever remembered how to walk properly when at last the time came.

It was a worrying and miserable day, and he felt cut off from his friends. He thought bitterly that people are very heartless towards cripples. They just don't care, he kept thinking, as if he really were one.

He was also a bit uneasy about Miss Blackett. She kept giving him strange looks, and talking about his foot – saying he must sit quite still and that she was not at all sure he ought to be at school at all.

One of the boys asked him if his foot were cut, and he said, in a brave sort of voice, 'Oh, not very badly.'

'Can I have a look?'

Mossy was in a panic. 'No,' he said crossly. 'You can *not* have a look. It might be catching. I think it's got germs on it.'

He was glad that Miss Blackett had not heard that conversation. It did not sound such a very good lie to him. He wondered how many he had told during the day.

After school, as he began to limp homewards, Octavius seemed at last to be sympathetic.

'You can come round and play after tea, if you like,' he said kindly.

'I'm afraid I don't feel up to it,' Mossy said in a weak, but brave voice. 'I'm rather tired. Perhaps I could come tomorrow.'

'Shall I come round to you?'

'I shall be going to bed, I think,' Mossy said.

'Well, I might just drop in and bring some comics for you. I'll give them to your mother.'

Mossy was alarmed. 'If you do, don't say anything to her about my foot, will you?' he pleaded.

'Why ever not?'

'It upsets her when it's mentioned,' Mossy said. He wondered if there could be anything as tiring as telling one lie after another. The first one was easy, but then they grew more and more difficult to invent.

He said goodbye to Octavius at the large, shabby house where he lived with all his brothers and sisters, and went limping on his way, in case anyone should see him. He was fairly sure that Octavius would forget about the comics. But he could not be quite sure. It would be safer to go to bed after tea. The whole affair was becoming both dangerous and boring.

He went straight up to his bedroom when he got home, and took off the black shoe and put on the brown one, and went downstairs walking ordinarily. It was a great relief. He had a good tea, and then told his mother that he thought he would like to go to bed.

She looked surprised.

'I just feel tired,' he said. 'I've had a hard day at school.' This was about the only true thing he had said that day.

'Well, the rest won't do you any harm,' she said. 'Doctor Primrose doesn't want you to get over-tired.' She knew because of the tea he had eaten, that there was nothing much wrong with him. He really did look tired, though; for all the acting he had done all day had worn him out.

I'm safe up here, Mossy told himself, looking round his bedroom and feeling dull, wondering how he could pass the long evening.

In case his mother came up, he had to get into bed. He had fetched some water from the bathroom, and he did some painting and messed up the sheet and pillow with all the colours of the rainbow, and a few more besides.

When it was dark, he knew that Octavius would not come. So he had wasted the evening for nothing. He put on his dressing-gown and went downstairs.

'I don't feel tired any longer,' he told his mother.

She looked at him suspiciously, but said that he could watch the television for half an hour. She really seemed quite glad of his company, as Father was out at a meeting in the village.

Mossy looked at the television and ate a banana and began to feel at peace. It was all over – that terrible day. Tomorrow, he would walk like other people, and go out to play at break, and tell the truth all day.

But the awful day was not over by a long way. Just as Mossy was going up to bed, Father came home. He looked angry.

As soon as he had closed the door, he asked Mossy, 'What is all this about catching your foot in a rabbit-trap?'

'A rabbit-trap?' Mother said, looking puzzled.

'Nothing,' Mossy mumbled. He knew this would not do, but he could think of nothing else to say.

'I saw Miss Blackett at the meeting and she sounded quite concerned and kept asking me questions, and I didn't know what the blazes she was talking about. I felt a complete idiot.'

'I'm sorry, Father.'

'You're sorry! I should jolly well think you *are* sorry. Telling a pack of deliberate lies, making fools of everyone.'

'I'm sorry,' Mossy said again, very quietly, tears pricking his eyes.

'I suppose you were trying to draw attention to yourself, as usual.'

The tears began to trickle down Mossy's cheeks. It was no use trying to explain, he thought, and he knew that he would really start to boo-hoo if he said much more. How could anyone possibly be expected to understand how it had all happened?

'But I don't understand . . .' Mother said. Father put up his hand to silence her. His face was red with temper. 'Switch that blessed television off,' he shouted, and Mossy quickly did so.

'Do you want everyone to think of you as a liar?' Father asked. 'Because that's what will happen, as sure as fate. Several of my friends were standing by. How do you think I felt?'

Mossy did not reply. He knew that his father was not really asking a question, but making a speech. In fact, there was no pause for an answer. The speech just went on and on.

Mossy rubbed his sleeve across his wet face, and stared down at the carpet with blurred eyes.

'Tomorrow, you will apologize to Miss Blackett,' his father was saying.

If only I could pass away! Mossy thought. If only I could be safely back in hospital, or in Australia. He wondered if he were too young to run away to sea.

'Well, your grandfather's coming on Saturday and

don't think for one moment that you'll be allowed to go out in the car with him. In any case, I doubt if he would want to take out such a naughty boy.'

'Father!' Mossy said in a desperate voice, lifting his tear-stained face at last. 'Please don't tell him why. Please don't! Just say I did something wrong. Don't say what.'

He felt that he could not bear his grandfather to know this sorry story, with all its silly ins-and-outs.

'I shall see how you behave between now and then,' Father said grimly. 'At this moment, you are to go to your room and get into bed, and I don't want to hear another word from you.'

Mossy went upstairs. He was dreading tomorrow, when he would have to apologize to Miss Blackett. He knew now that she hadn't believed him about his foot, and that she had mentioned it to Father to make sure. He was furious with her for not believing him. He was in a black mood against his father, too. He would have liked to draw them both on the wall, with huge, red, angry faces.

Instead, he pulled out the top drawer of the chest and, on the side of it, where he thought it would never be seen he drew the nastiest face he could for Miss Blackett, with crooked teeth and spots all over her, and hair like a mop, and his father with a long nose and crossed eyes, and fleas the size of bumble-bees swarming out of his fuzzy hair. Then he slid the drawer back, and felt better.

He got into bed and pulled up the sheet with all the paint daubed over it. It seemed in another life that he had done that. He would, no doubt, get into trouble for it, but it would only be a small trouble of the kind that he could bear.

He put out the light and closed his eyes, and tried not to think about tomorrow. A miracle might happen in the night. He might wake up in the morning to find that he had caught mumps from Selwyn.

Downstairs, Father was still in a bad mood.

'Where that boy of yours gets it from, I simply can't think,' he told Mother.

'I don't know where that boy of *yours* gets it from either,' she said quietly.

He ignored her remark, and then asked, 'Were *you* naughty at school?'

'A little,' she said cautiously.

'In what way?' He was stern, as if she were a small child, and he was her school-teacher.

'I spoke in a corridor,' she confessed. 'In those days, which Emma calls "old-fashioned", we weren't allowed to do that.'

'Well, it's not very bad,' he said, almost as if he were disappointed.

'I also slid down some banisters.'

'That's a little better ... I mean, a bit worse.'

'And I ... I ...' She was trying to remember something really dreadful, as it seemed to be the only way of cheering him up.

'There, there,' he said gently, putting an arm round her. 'I shan't punish you, you know.'

He was still puzzled though. He still did not know where Mossy's bad ways had come from – and come from somewhere they must have done. He had been very good at school, although he thought it himself. He began to wonder about Grandfather. Perhaps it was his fault. He now remembered distinctly his father saying, 'Poor old Gertie always said I was a holy terror.' Once that was settled in his mind, he felt better.

As he had not had the luck to wake up with mumps, the next morning, with a burning hot face, Mossy went up to Miss Blackett and said, in a low voice, 'I'm very sorry about yesterday.'

'As long as you're better,' she said with a sarcastic smile.

Time heals all, he told himself.

10

The New-Born Baby

On Saturday, Grandfather arrived with Fortnum to
stay for a day or two. When he suggested taking Mossy
for the usual drive, Father said, 'I'm sorry, Dad, but
that's all off. I told him he couldn't, as a punishment.
There's been a bit of bother, but we needn't go into
that.'

Mossy was greatly relieved that they needn't. And
the car had its hood up now for the winter, so the drive
would not have been as much fun as usual.

He was feeling more cheerful by now. It seemed to be
true about time healing all – though it is never easy to
believe it at the time of a disaster. Of course, he could
imagine some kinds of disaster that time could never
heal. If Mother died, for instance. He could never get
over *that*, he thought, not if he lived to be a hundred

years old. Tears came into his eyes and his nose tingled as if he were going to sneeze, but the sneeze refused to come.

'What's the matter, Mossy?' his mother asked.

'Nothing,' he said. It was only a white lie, he thought, told so as not to hurt someone else's feelings. He could not very well explain to his mother that he was imagining her dead.

'Are you quite sure?'

'Quite sure.' He smiled. The awful thought had gone, and he was happy again. 'I just thought I was going to sneeze,' he said.

He knew that his mother was looking at him very carefully these days, and that what she was looking for was signs of mumps. She kept staring at his face, and stroking him behind the ears and under his chin, gently cupping his face in her hands. It would be the last straw, she said to Grandfather, if Mossy should get mumps just now. It was bad enough as it was, wondering who could look after the children when she went into the hospital to have the baby.

'I can stay and look after them,' Grandfather said.

Mother gave a very small smile – as if this were just a joke, and not a particularly funny one.

'I mean it,' Grandfather insisted.

'It's sweet of you,' she said, 'but how could you?'

'Perfectly well. I've looked after children before now.

Used to do quite a lot for Robert, when poor old Gertie was ill.'

Robert was Mossy's father. Mossy tried to imagine him as a little boy, and Grandfather, much younger than now, giving him a bath. It was impossible. However hard he tried to picture it, Grandfather still looked the same, and Father was wearing his moustache. Mossy could make him small in his imagination, so that he was quite a little baby sitting up in the bath and playing with a floating duck, like Emma's – but he could not get rid of the moustache, or think of Father at any time without it.

Meanwhile, the discussion was going on about whether Grandfather could look after them or not. Mossy hoped that he would be allowed to.

'Of course I can do it,' Grandfather kept saying. 'We'll have a high old time.'

Perhaps this was what Mother was afraid of, for she looked worried.

Father was all in favour of the plan. He said that between them they could manage very well.

Apart from Emma, who wasn't listening, but was talking to herself as usual, they all wanted it – Mossy thought it would be great fun, and he longed for this high old time that was promised. Father would prefer it to having Miss Silkin, or someone of the kind, hanging about the house all the time. Grandfather, more than

any of them, wanted it. He would enjoy the change. Although he had a lot of friends, and Fortnum, he had sometimes been lonely since poor old Gertie died. He loved coming down to the country to be with them all. But he never stayed long, because he said that Robert and Laura had their own lives to lead.

Father had been doing some carpentry, and Emma had picked up the curly wood-shavings and had stuck them in her hair so that they looked like ringlets. Or she thought they did. She was walking about very gently, so that they should not drop out of her hair, and she was pretending to be a princess.

'Well, is it "yes" or "no"?' Grandfather asked. 'You'd like me to come and stay with you, wouldn't you?' he asked Emma.

'You *are* here,' she said.

'We can open the odd tin of beans,' Father was saying to Mother. 'I can see to breakfast and get Emma up, before I go to work.'

'We shan't exist entirely on tins of beans, you know,' Grandfather said. 'I've a few cooking tricks up my sleeve. As no doubt Robert could tell you.'

Suddenly, Mother's face lost its worried look and she smiled. 'Very well,' she said. 'I see no reason why not. You're a kind darling.' She got up and put her arms round Grandfather and kissed him.

'That's all settled,' he said, patting her hand fondly.

'I really have been worried,' she confessed. 'I couldn't sleep for wondering what was the best thing to do.'

'*This* is the best thing,' Father said.

'Much the best thing,' said Mossy.

The next morning, while Grandfather was still with them, Mother came back from answering the telephone, looking quite excited.

'Vera's bringing Herbert to see us this afternoon,' she said – as if this were one of the greatest treats she could be promised. 'I'm dying to see what he's like.'

'Who's Vera?' Grandfather asked. 'Not that Silkin woman?'

Mother looked at him reproachfully. He often spoke rudely and set a bad example, but she could not scold him. He was so kind to her, and she was fond of him.

'She's a very old friend of mine,' she said. 'And she's engaged to be married, to a man she met on holiday. It's so romantic.'

'And he is this Herbert?' Grandfather asked.

'Yes, I really can't imagine him. I've only seen a photograph. Well, they're coming to tea, so we shall see.'

Off she hurried to the larder, as Mossy knew she would, and out came the flour and sugar and butter and the little tin with the caraway seeds in it. Doesn't she *ever* get tired of that horrible cake? Mossy wondered.

In the early part of the afternoon, he and Grandfather went for a walk on the common with Fortnum, who dashed in and out of the bushes excitedly, his tongue flapping and his tail wagging. The country was a great treat to him, after the hard, plain streets of London, where he always had to be on a lead.

Mossy told Grandfather about Alison and how she had fallen out of the tree, and that they were both to be train-bearers at Miss Silkin's wedding.

'You seem to have changed your mind about that wedding,' Grandfather said.

'I don't mind now I know what Alison's like.'

'What *is* she like?'

Mossy thought for a moment, and then said, 'Well, she's not ugly, but she's not pretty, either. It's a funny sort of face. She keeps screwing it up, and puffing out her cheeks. She's not too tall and she's not too short. Some of her teeth have come out. She walks with a limp – well, she did when I saw her, because she had just fallen out of the tree. Perhaps she doesn't now. She wears tights. What else can I say? I think she has small eyes, but not too small, and her ears stick out, but not very much.'

'She sounds a real charmer,' Grandfather said.

'Perhaps I don't make her sound very nice,' Mossy said doubtfully.

'She comes across to me O.K.,' Grandfather said.

'And I suppose we'll be in the usual black books if we don't make for home.' He whistled to Fortnum, who jumped out of some bushes, with bits of dry bracken sticking to him. He was a dog who really seemed sometimes to be laughing. Mongrels are better at this than other kinds of dogs.

'Now for Herbert!' Grandfather said.

Outside the house was a large, black car. It looked as though Herbert might be rich.

Inside, Miss Silkin was blushing and smiling. She was all beads and teeth. Her necklace, Mossy thought, was like rows and rows of baked beans.

Herbert was fat, and wore a suit with a very large check pattern and a red waistcoat and a green tie. Perhaps he was colour-blind, Mossy thought, and so had no clue as to what he was wearing. There seemed to be no other explanation for such a mixture. His purple cheeks, of course, he could not help.

'My dear little Mossy,' Miss Silkin said, introducing him. She had never called him anything like that before. 'Our page-boy,' she added, patting Mossy's head.

'Yours, my dear,' said Herbert. 'He won't be doing much for me.'

'Oh, Herbert, you *are* a tease,' she said. 'He's simply terrible to me,' she went on, looking at Mother and smiling more than ever.

'Why do you want to marry him, then?' Mossy asked.

Then Mother said 'Shush!' and all the others except Miss Silkin laughed – Herbert and Grandfather especially. Miss Silkin, in the end, managed a little trill, but looked annoyed.

They began tea. Emma tried everything and finished nothing. When it was just family, she was not allowed to do this; but, although she was so young, she had realized that Mother did not like making a fuss in front of visitors; so, while she could get away with it, she did – giving bits of sandwiches to Fortnum when she thought no one was looking (Mother was, but pretended she wasn't) and nibbling the corners off biscuits.

Miss Silkin looked disapproving, and Mossy stared her out, because he felt it was Mother's and Father's business to bring up their children, and no one else's – especially someone who had never had to do it.

Then he suddenly thought that Miss Silkin and Herbert (Mr Boot, as he was) might one day have children of their own, and the idea so much amused him that he nearly choked when he was drinking some milk. He was glad he would not have to be one of them.

The honeymoon was being discussed. They were going to Madeira, which Mossy thought was the name of a cake. He thought it would be nice if there were a place called Seedy they could go to instead. It would be a very small, dry, dull, shabby and old-fashioned place, and Herbert wouldn't like it much, as he apparently didn't like the cake of that name, for he kept on taking another slice of the shop one, instead of Mother's. He had a good appetite, and looked as if he had had it for a long time.

Mother was asking Grandfather if he would like some more tea.

'No, thank you, my dear. I'm not much of a one for tea, as you know. Something stronger a little later, eh, Herbert?'

Herbert looked delighted. He and Grandfather were getting on like a house on fire, and Miss Silkin was looking glum as if it were *her* house that was burning. She kept trying to change their conversations.

It was amazing to Mossy that Herbert should still want to marry her, for he seemed quite a cheerful person. Mossy hoped, now, that he would not change his mind; for then it would be more than likely that he would never see Alison again.

When they had gone, Grandfather helped Mother with the washing-up, as if to prove to her how good he would be at house-work when she was in hospital.

'Well, she's got *him* hooked,' Mossy heard him say. He did not quite understand what this meant. It sounded like someone having caught a fish, and he amused himself by picturing Miss Silkin on a river-bank, while

Herbert splashed about in the water at the end of her line.

Mother said that this was not a very nice expression for Grandfather to have used about her friend.

'She'll soon take the smile off his face,' Grandfather went on, taking no notice.

Mother did not like some of the things he said, but this time she said nothing.

Then there was a crash. Something fell and broke on the kitchen floor.

'Well, I'm blessed,' said Grandfather, sounding really astonished. 'It simply slipped out of my hand.'

'Never mind,' Mother said, in rather a tired voice. 'You go and sit down, and I'll finish this.'

In the middle of the night, Mossy was awakened by someone quietly shutting the front door. Then he heard whispers, and footsteps on the garden path, going away from the house, and the car being started up and driven away.

As he was listening to it getting fainter and fainter in the distance, he fell asleep again.

The next time he was awakened, it was by Grandfather. Mother had gone to the hospital in the night, he said, and Father was with her, so they had to manage by themselves.

Mossy got up and dressed himself, and went downstairs. Emma was already up, and looked rather funny because Grandfather had put her dress on the wrong way round.

In the middle of breakfast, when Mossy was feeling very strange, just being there alone with Grandfather and Emma, Father came back.

'It's a boy,' he shouted through the letter-box, while he was trying to find his key. Mossy ran to open the door. His father looked tired, and his chin was dark because he had not shaved. He also looked very pleased and excited.

Emma began to wail, because she had wanted a sister; but she soon cheered up and became as happy as everyone else.

Father drank a cup of tea, and then went upstairs to shave and get ready for work. It was a special day to all of them.

When Mossy had gone to school, Emma went into the garden. She leaned over the gate in her back-to-front dress, and to everyone who passed by she said, 'I had a new-born baby last night.'

Grandfather proved to be quite a cook. It came a usual thing to Mossy to find him, with his shirt-sleeves rolled up, wearing one of Mother's aprons, stirring something at the stove. He made really wonderful what he called 'fun-food' – bits of meat on skewers, hot, melted-cheese they dipped pieces of bread into, toasted marshmallows, toffee-apples. Sometimes they tossed and flopped pancakes about the kitchen, and had the high old time he'd promised them. He could also do magic-cooking – for instance, a pudding brought out of a very hot oven, with cold ice-cream inside it.

It all took Father back a year or two.

Sometimes they had stomach-ache, but didn't care.

Emma made gingerbread men for Mossy's tea, and Mossy envied her being with Grandfather all day, cooking and having fun, while he was at school.

'You're a good, adventurous eater,' Grandfather told Mossy. 'I like that in a boy. Try anything, I always say. Even if you never want it again.'

Mother heard all about their adventurous eating when Father went to see her in the evenings in hospital.

'Oh, dear! He didn't give Emma *curry*!' she said.

She could not help worrying about what was going on at home. Although she loved Grandfather, she always found him rather a strain, not knowing what he would be up to next. But he had most certainly come to the rescue, and soon she would be home again, and get them back to their plain and proper meals.

The time went quite quickly. Mossy had enjoyed all the novelty, but he knew that he would not have liked it to last forever.

Then the day came when Mother brought the new baby home. It was a sunny Saturday morning, and Father was there, and waiting for the time to come when he could go and fetch her.

They had made the house as tidy as they could, and put bunches of flowers around the place.

Mossy hung about, waiting for the car to come back. When it did, he rushed to the gate. Mother got out of the car, holding the new baby rolled up in a white shawl. She looked quite different. He had forgotten what she had looked like before the baby had begun to be on the way.

Grandfather flung open the front door, and stood there, wearing one of Mother's aprons, and waving a wooden spoon. 'Welcome home!' he shouted. Mother kissed him, and went into the house, sniffing suspiciously, for Grandfather was cooking lunch, and she wondered what the smell could be.

'It's an old Arab recipe,' Grandfather explained. 'Poor old Gertie's father brought it back from the Middle East.'

'Oh, I see,' Mother said quietly, full of foreboding.

When she sat down, with the baby in her arms, they could have a better look at him. Mother drew back the shawl and showed them.

He was sleeping peacefully, with one little mauve hand folded by his face. He had the tiniest fingernails imaginable, and his forehead was furrowed and frowning, like some puzzled old man's.

Mossy looked at him in wonder. A real person. No longer on the way, but here, arrived.

'This is little William,' Mother told Emma, putting an arm round her and hugging her.

Emma peeped inside the shawl, then looked up at her mother, beaming.

'Can I play with it?' she asked. She could just fancy herself, putting the baby to bed in a cardboard-box, dressing and undressing him, and brushing his dark, fluffy hair. It would be a great improvement on those games when she had to make believe that Bunty was a baby.

'Not till he's stronger,' Mother said.

'When will that be?'

'One of these days.'

'Tomorrow?'

'No, not tomorrow.'

Emma pouted. 'Why is he so weak?' she asked.

'He's just very tiny.'

As far as Mossy was concerned, it would be years, he knew, if ever, before this new brother would be of any use to him.

All the same, as he went off to see if he could find Octavius or someone to keep him company, he realized that this baby had made a difference to him. He was the eldest of three now. The eldest son. He looked down at his shadow on the road, and it seemed to him that it had grown longer. And even little Emma had gone up one. Although she could never be the eldest, like him, she wasn't the baby any more. They were all more important than they had been.

11

The Wedding

Now it was dark winter. All the leaves had fallen, and the trees were just scribble.

Grandfather had long ago gone home, and the baby was part of the family now, as if he had almost always been there. Mossy was used to his crying, and to seeing napkins airing all round the kitchen.

He – Mossy – had not caught mumps, and Selwyn was better, and now the wedding was the thing to think about.

The kilt was ready, and the new buckled shoes. When the day came, Selwyn's mother, Mrs Noah, was to have the baby and give him his bottle and mind him, so that Mother could go to the wedding. Emma was going, too, and had some new red shoes; but she was only going to look on, Mossy thought – not to take part, as he and Alison would.

On the wedding morning the four of them were to drive up to London, and Mossy would change into his finery at Alison's house – so that the kilt would not be crumpled up by the journey. Miss Silkin would be there, too, changing into *her* finery. It was her sister's house and had more room than her own.

When the day came, Mossy woke up early and went to look out of the window to see what sort of morning it was. It was *so* early that it was not really any sort of morning at all yet. The sky had no colour and everything looked very wintry.

Rooks were flying into the top of a big elm tree he could see. They came homing quickly back, hurrying in twos and threes, like people trying to get to church before the slow bell stopped ringing. The noise was terrible. At last, they were all up in the tree, and the branches seemed to rock with the weight of them. Mossy tried to count them, but they were shifting about, as if they were trying to find more comfortable perches. Soon they were settled, and seemed to be having a meeting, and now the bare tree looked like a spotted veil. Mossy stood by the window and stared, and wondered what the meeting could be about.

He jumped when he heard his mother's voice behind him. 'You'll catch your death of cold,' she said. The rooks seemed to jump, too. Suddenly, they lifted their wings and scattered in all directions, and the tree was empty again.

'You must get dressed now,' Mother said, and Mossy turned from the window, and began to take off his pyjamas.

He was too nervous and excited to eat much breakfast, and all the way to London he kept having sudden shivers of alarm.

Alison's house was in a quiet, dull road, which looked as if nothing exciting had ever happened in it.

Alison opened the door to them. She was not limping any more, but she had a big, red graze on her forehead. She had fallen out of something else, she explained. This time it was a climbing-frame in the park.

Mossy stared at her and decided that she was just as nice-looking as he had remembered.

Inside the house, it was all bustle and confusion. A cold lunch was laid on a table in the dining-room for people to help themselves to, as they pleased, and some were already dressed in their wedding-clothes and others were hanging about waiting to get into the bathroom, where Miss Silkin had been locked for nearly an hour.

Alison's mother, who was quite unlike her sister, but rather strict-looking, took them to have some lunch. It would be fatal, she said, if Alison were to eat anything once she had changed into her bridesmaid's dress. She had already made a mess of her face, but she need not make a mess of her clothes.

While they were eating, she told them exactly what they had to do in the church, and said they would have a little practice when Miss Silkin came downstairs.

'*When*,' she said again, with a sigh.

Somehow, the time went by. Mossy put on the kilt and the new shoes, which Mother had made him wear a little at home, so that they would not be uncomfortable on the day. She kept trying to smooth his hair, but the bit on top stuck up as usual, wedding or no wedding.

Two older bridesmaids suddenly appeared, coming downstairs together, dressed in blue.

Miss Silkin still did not appear, so one of the tall bridesmaids pinned a tablecloth to the back of her dress, and made Alison and Mossy pretend it was a train and follow her all round the room, holding it.

At last, it was time to go to the church. Miss Silkin would come last of all, with Alison's father, who was giving her away.

The two older bridesmaids and Alison and Mossy went off in a car together. The church was not far away, and when they got there, they stood in the porch and shivered, and waited for the bride.

Alison wore a white dress, with little blue rosebuds on it, and a blue ribbon round her waist, and a wreath

of blue and white flowers on her head. The wreath kept slipping crooked, and had to be put right by one or other of the big bridesmaids. The graze on her forehead looked very unbridesmaid-like, and she told Mossy that Miss Silkin had been quite annoyed with her when she had fallen off the climbing-frame, and had not even enquired if she were hurt.

The only times we're together, Mossy thought, we have to waste them. The first time, because she had hurt her leg, and now with all this dressed-up nonsense. If only he could have a long, long day with her, and take her on the common, and show her the rubbish dump, and the hollow tree, and other hiding-places.

At last, Miss Silkin arrived. She stood in the porch, looking nervous and rather ghostly, Mossy thought. The big bridesmaids re-arranged her veil, and they all took up their positions, and the organ began to play the Wedding March.

'Here comes the bride,' Mossy whispered to Alison, as they lifted up the train.

'All fat and wide,' she whispered back.

'Keep the proper distance from me,' hissed Miss Silkin over her shoulder. Then, walking slowly, they entered the church and the people in the pews turned their heads round slightly to see the bride.

Herbert was waiting, standing there, on his best behaviour.

The Service began. Mossy stood very still, hoping it would not go on too long, but soon Alison was fidgeting. The wreath of flowers had slipped sideways again and she kept stooping down to pull up her socks. One of the big bridesmaids behind them tapped her on the shoulder.

Perhaps one day, Mossy thought, when they were

grown up, he would be standing with Alison beside him, in front, where Miss Silkin and Herbert were.

'I Herbert, take thee, Vera, to my wedded wife,' Herbert repeated loudly after the clergyman.

Surely, Mossy thought, a wife *has* to be wedded. It had always seemed to him to be the point about *being* a wife.

('I, Mossy, take thee, Alison, to my wedded wife.')

He tried it out in his mind, and then thought that, on such an occasion, he would be using his first name of Robert, like his father.

They sang a hymn, and Alison, not knowing the words, looked about her, and turned her head round to smile at people she knew, and the older bridesmaid tapped her on the shoulder again. Mossy kept his head still, and only looked at Alison from the corners of his eyes.

Soon it was over, and they were making the return journey down the aisle, and wedding bells could be heard on the frosty air outside.

They all went to have a party in a big hotel and Alison picked up her long skirt and whooped about, and the flower-wreath finally fell off.

Mossy could not help still thinking of the bride as Miss Silkin, although she would never be that again, but Mrs Boot. She had never been the sort of person to be called by her Christian name by many people, and

Mossy thought that she would probably always be Miss Silkin to him.

The reception – as the hotel party was called – was quite fun, except for some rather long speeches. One of them was about how charming and lovely Miss Silkin had always been, and what a lucky fellow Herbert should consider himself.

Mossy and Alison were left to themselves and sat in a dark corner and ate one little dish of trifle after another. Alison spilled some orange squash on the white tablecloth, and was pleased that she would not

have to cover *that* stain with pennies. She had also spilled the orange squash on her dress, and hoped that there would not be trouble about that.

The minute that the bride and bridegroom had gone off in the car to the airport, on their way to Madeira, Mother told Mossy that they must be on their way home. She was beginning to fret about the baby and longed to collect him from Mrs Noah's.

It was hard saying goodbye to Alison, and Mossy was very quiet, lolling back in the dark car, going over in his mind all that had happened.

'Well, that really *was* a wedding,' Mother said. Mossy supposed that she would talk of it for days, telling each different person the same old things.

'Ridiculous waste of money,' Father said.

Lights from shop-windows flashed into the car. The streets were very empty. It was a cold, dark Saturday evening.

'How lovely to be in Madeira,' Mother said wistfully.

Father hated her to be wistful, so he said sharply that it was the last place he wanted to go to.

'Mother,' Mossy said in a rather wavering, uncertain voice. 'Will I ever see Alison again?' He hated to ask, but had to know. Children are in the power of grown-ups. They are too young to make difficult plans, or arrange things for themselves.

'I'm sure you will,' she said in her comfortable way,

but as if she were not really paying much attention.

'Yes, but how?'

'We can ask Herbert and Vera to bring her when they come to see us.'

'When?'

'When they're back from their honeymoon and settled down.'

'But when will that be?'

'Oh, really, Mossy! How do I know? In the summer, I dare say.'

But the summer was ages away. They were in the depths of winter, and had not even had Christmas yet.

He lay back, with his eyes shut, feeling sad. The summer! he thought. What a beautiful word it was! It suggested sun and the humming of bees. The cherry-blossom would come out again, and fall, and the common would turn golden with gorse and all the tiny fists of bracken would uncurl. The cuckoo would call from tree to tree. There would be everything he loved, and Alison to show it to.

Emma had fallen asleep, and Mossy was almost doing the same. As he dozed off, he could see the picture of them both, himself and Alison, running and leaping in the bracken, with the sun pouring down, and the birds singing.

THURSDAY'S CHILDREN

Rumer Godden

Doone Penny is a child with a gist – he was born to dance. Although others recognise his talent, there is little encouragement from his family. His mother preens over his pretty sister, Crystal, also a dancer, but fiercely competitive and vain. Doone's father would never allow a son of *his* to have ballet lessons, and his brothers think he's a sissy. But Doone has passion and ambition beyond his years, and knows he can succeed, if only he is given the chance. If he can make it into Queen's Chase, Her Majesty's Junior Ballet School, he'll show them all . . .

'*A tale of ambition . . . Aspirational, exciting and moving*'
Adèle Geras

'*I've always adored Rumer Godden. She writes beautifully and creates such distinctive, realistic children*'
Jacqueline Wilson

JANE OF LANTERN HILL

L. M. Montgomery

Jane and her mother live in a gloomy old mansion where their lives are ruled by her overbearing grandmother. Jane has always believed that her father is dead. Then, one dull April morning, a letter comes. Not only is her father alive and well, but he wants Jane to spend the summer with him on Prince Edward Island.

For a blissful summer she lives at her father's cottage on Lantern Hill, making friends, having adventures and discovering that life can be wonderful after all. And she dares to dream that there could be such a house where she and her parents could live together with Grandmother's disapproval – a house that could be called home.

RILLA OF INGLESIDE

L. M. Montgomery

Anne Shirley's children are almost all grown up – except for
pretty, high-spirited Rilla, who is almost fifteen years old.
Rilla's thoughts are filled with going to her first dance at the
Four Winds lighthouse – and getting her very first kiss from
a handsome Kenneth Ford.

But at the dance, news is announced that England has
declared war on Germany. At first, this means little to Rilla,
on the threshold of so many new excitements. But as her
brothers go off to fight in the Great War and Rilla brings
home an orphaned newborn baby in a soup tureen, she is
swept into a drama that tests her courage and will leave her
changed for ever . . .